To E
Rol

Colin.

A CERTAIN
CHEMISTRY

Short stories bubbling
with life - and death

Colin Evans

Etive Independent Publishing

ISBN-13: 9798273610903
ISBN-10: 1477123456

Cover design by: Etive Independent
Library of Congress Control Number: 2018675309
Printed in the United States of America

Dedicated to all book lovers -
particularly my wife Fi

CONTENTS

INTRODUCTION

by Colin Evans

A good short story crosses the borders of our nations and our prejudices and our beliefs. A good short story asks a question that can't be answered in simple terms. And even if we come up with some understanding, years later, while glancing out of a window, the story still has the potential to return, to alter right there in our mind and change everything.— Walter Mosley

L IKE many, I love to get my teeth into a good book. Recently I read and became thoroughly immersed in Hilary Mantel's Wolf Hall series. They are massive tomes with sometimes complex themes. No chance, nor indeed no wish, to skim over them. But I've also discovered a liking for short stories via the starkly contrasting and, yet somehow similar writings of Ernest Hemingway and the American crime novelist Elmore Leonard. I began trying my luck with the rapidly proliferating short story competitions, did okay, and so have progressed to this, my first anthology.

Dear reader – a warning. It is experimental. There is no running theme, apart from the fact that the stories were originally written as entries to various competitions between 2024 and 2025. As such they had to conform to competition rules in terms of content and length – ranging from 50 words to 4,000 - some having to include a given 'prompt'. Most draw on real life situations with numerous autobiographical hints, particularly alluding to my experience as a journalist and, in retirement, as a family historian.

There is a lot of crime, some refer to events in India where my wife and I have enjoyed wonderful times, and some recall an era before instant communications when journalists were allowed too much rope (and sometimes hanged themselves!). Some are 'gritty', even dark, others (hopefully) contain sparks of humour. I admit to an occasional cross-over of fact and fiction – it is for the reader to discern where – and to a little vague repetition where the basis for one story has been amended for another to suit a different competition. Into the mix I've thrown in some essays on various self-chosen topics.

Short story writing, sometimes called Flash Fiction, is a skill which I'm still learning. Some might think that it's much easier to write a tale of 1,000 words than a novel of 90,000. In some ways, it is. But, usually, the novelist has time and space to fatten and embellish words, phrases, sentences, paragraphs. A short story demands rigid discipline. Each word rated for value. Particularly when having to adhere to certain restrictions. It's a challenge, but a worthwhile one because I believe it encourages creative writing and, as important, creative reading. You can't skim a story told in 50 words. It hits you hard, makes you wonder. At least that's the objective. Whatever the content or length, a short story should entertain and/or provoke. An essay of which there are four here, must at least inform. Hopefully, the following selection complies. To help the reader understand the context better, a brief explanation of how and why accompanies each piece and there are notes at the back of the book.

The anthology takes its title from the opening story which was short-listed for the 2024 H G Wells Prize. Thank you for buying/sharing this book. I hope you enjoy it.

A CERTAIN CHEMISTRY

(Short-listed for the 2024 H G Wells Short Story Prize, max words 3,500 - written under the competition prompt of 'The Fool')

THE exam paper challenged me to a fight. A slight crease on the page resembled a frown, admonishing my lack of respect for the subject, as well as my ignorance of it. I wrote my name, school, and date at the top. No point in anything else. Chemistry wasn't my scene. I'd learned little about it except how to use a Bunsen burner to scorch my initials into a worktop. Perversely, I'd relished every minute in the laboratory. Our teacher, Mr Wilson, cracked us up.

The school was brand new and incomplete, a reflection of the 1960s' era, so that the glass in the high, wide classroom windows was criss-crossed with red tape and marked in black felt tip as FRAGILE. Mr Wilson warned us with a pointed finger: "Do NOT bang the door - it could cause the glass to fall out. DO NOT BANG THE DOOR!" One or two giggled. It was difficult to take him seriously. Already, in the few hours we had known him, he had displayed a pleasing array of idiosyncrasies. Easily flustered, his face reddened, and saliva dribbled from the corner of his mouth.

On his way out, Mr Wilson banged the door and, not surprisingly, the windows capsized, the glass falling slowly, then shattering into thousands of tiny pieces. As his suede Hush Puppies crunched through the shrapnel he muttered: "See what I mean."

Calamity after calamity dogged his footsteps. The 'lab' was full of joy as well as foul-smelling fumes and unregulated flames. We dived to the floor clutching our throats, claiming to be poisoned, or staggered towards the door, faces smeared with charcoal, shouting 'Fire, fire!' Vivid green and blue liquids, deliberately over-heated, frothed out of glass bowls to form wondrous bubbling streams which melted anything in their path. He often lost his temper, his cherubic cheeks growing deep crimson, white flecks on his lips and his words sticking at the back of his throat.

His lack of control extended beyond the classroom. He wore odd socks. His tweed tie was permanently twisted to one side, pushing his shirt collar askew. While looking after the VIPs at the school's inaugural sports day he tripped headlong over a rope, spilling a tray of drinks into the laps of the town's Mayor and his pretty teenage daughter who was acting as his consort. Panicking, Mr Wilson pulled out a white hankie and tried to wipe the girl down, only to be hauled off by the Head who had rushed in like a hawk, his black gown billowing behind him.

"Fool," he hissed.

No wonder we all looked forward to Wilson's lessons, but, of course, when it came to the GCE exams I didn't have a clue.

After leaving school I came across him twice more.

On the first occasion I was working for the Local Rag, covering the school's Speech Day. Afterwards, supping a pint in a nearby pub, I spotted a clutch of teachers standing near the fireplace. They called me over.

"Collins, isn't it?" said Mr Wilson. "Always messing about at the back of the class. Wasn't there some trick you pulled with a Bunsen burner?" He glanced around his circle of colleagues, expecting encouragement, but they were mute, vaguely embarrassed. "Well, yes," he stuttered, "a long time ago, eh?"

"Yes," I said, lightly. "I'm married now. But I'm quite handy with a gas stove." The art teacher Miss Chamberlain tried to stifle a laugh but succeeded only in spurting Babycham over the back of her hand. Mr Wilson adjusted his collar. Sweating profusely from the heat of the fire, a lank of fair hair flopping over his forehead and with a glass of ale in his fist, he reminded me of Kingsley Amis's character Lucky Jim.

But 'Jim' survived and prospered despite himself. He was the type who could unwittingly miss a red traffic light without hitting anyone or causing a pile-up, whereas Mr Wilson would smash into a bunch of pedestrians.

Over 40 years later I bumped into him again. This time on a wild, tiny island, 30 miles into the Atlantic. We holidayed there regularly, and I was whiling away a rain-lashed day in the rickety community centre when the door flew open, rattling the windows, to reveal an elderly man, ill-dressed for the weather in a lightweight suit. Grey, thinning hair and thick-rimmed specs. He stood for a moment, blinking, unsure of what to do until urged forward by a command from behind, a woman's voice, exasperated. "Go in and sit down for God's sake!" She pulled up a chair and plonked him in it, pushing down on his shoulders. She stood on guard, arms folded, harassed. His wife, I assumed. And his carer.

Mr Wilson started chatting, his head swivelling around to take in the surroundings, an old piano, shelves loaded with second-hand paperbacks, a chess table. I didn't recognise him initially, but he looked familiar and as he rambled on, the memories flooded back.

"Wonderful," he exclaimed, squinting up at me. "Wonderful. You organise things here, do you? Yes, we need to get things organised..." He was levering himself up only to be shoved back down by his bodyguard, a cloud of irritation crossing her face. "Yes, you see," he continued gamely, "I was a science teacher. Science is about organising things and…"

Behind him, Mrs Wilson rolled her eyes.

"I'm sure the gentleman isn't interested and has lots of things to do," she told him testily. She was younger, once attractive but battle-hardened, tired, and edgy. Time for my exit.

"Nice meeting you Mr Wilson. I was one of your pupils, you know. Collins." Surprised, his wife stared hard. But he showed no reaction. Suddenly he lunged from the chair, grabbing hold of the chess table for balance, and scattering the pieces on the floor. Mrs Wilson groaned and hauled him back. "Will you be alright?" I asked her, over his head.

"Yes. We're only here for the weekend. And anyway, I'm used to it. Is there somewhere here where I can get a glass of water? It's time for his meds."

I left a few minutes later. He'd swallowed his pills, grimacing. Going out I glanced back to see her sit down wearily, scanning her watch. I remembered to close the door gently.

Next day, the storm had blown out, bringing forth a golden autumn afternoon. I ambled around the sandy coastal path, gorse and bracken interspersed with broken rock formations, and nearing full circle, saw a movement on the other side of a large granite boulder.

"Oh, hello again."

She sat in the shade, overlooking the horse-shoe bay, gazing towards America, a cigarette dangling from her hand. Shielding her eyes she looked up, said: "It's a small world, isn't it? Especially on an island like this," and took a long drag. Considering her mood the previous afternoon, I was pleased she took my sudden appearance so serenely. Maybe it was the tobacco, perhaps the absence of her husband.

"Mr Wilson not around?"

"No. He's having a nap. He has lots of naps." She glanced up again. "Why don't you park yourself?" She patted the waterproof she had spread across the ground. "Smoke?"

"No, thanks. Never have."

"Good for you. I only took it up a few years ago. Funny, when I was young, I would never have dreamed of it. Now I get through 10 a day without any problem. Keeps me sane - along with the odd glass or two."

"Babycham, if I remember right."

"Babycham?! Not now, I need something a tad stronger - and how do you know that?" I dragged her back to the scene in the pub. "Ah yes. That's the night he proposed. Made a mess of it, of course, but sweet, really." And the former Miss Chamberlain smiled, the corners of her eyes crinkling. "Yes, he got down on his knees, very romantic, but then fell sideways. Too much Dutch courage. Still, it's the thought that counts."

As a gentle tide rolled in, seals cavorted in the shallows, huge black-backed gulls screeched overhead, and a flock of cormorants splashed down confident of a good feed. The water covered outlying rocks, then mudflats, and began to impinge on the sand, white for most of the day but now alchemised into a golden strand by the low October sun.

She pulled her knees up tight, resting her chin on them.

"Wouldn't you like to get it onto canvas?" I asked, gesturing towards the shimmering sea.

"No. Well, yes, of course. But you need energy for painting. It might seem a sedentary occupation, sitting there in front of an easel, but if you put everything into it, rather than merely being satisfied with something 'nice', it can leave you exhausted. It's heart and soul stuff, as far as I'm concerned and I just haven't got anything left."

Bitter? Resigned? Both, I guessed. But she wasn't for dwelling on it.

"October," said Mrs Wilson, breathing out a ring of smoke. "A lovely time of year. We always get away at half-term. It's one of the few things he recalls. At least it was until we met you."

Stamping the cigarette out on a pebble, she shoved the stub back into the packet, wrapped her arms around herself and rocked a little. I remained quiet. She half-turned towards me. "It's bizarre, isn't it? His memory collapsed years ago - along with everything else - but we come here, this pinhead of the British Isles, meet one of his ex-pupils, and, would you believe it, he's raking up the good old days, whenever they were. Kept me awake all night, rabbiting on. You've obviously triggered something in him."

A memory: Mr Wilson denouncing me as a 'coffee bar cowboy' and throwing a piece of string at me to tie up my hair, although he had the grace to apologise. "You lot," he said, tugging at his tie. "You'd make a saint swear. I'm sorry, Collins, it's just that you're the type that brings out the devil in me."

Now, it seemed, I had again unwittingly acted as a bottle-opener. I wondered how much more might be revealed. "Tell me to mind my own business if you want but, erm, what's wrong with him? Dementia?" She changed the subject abruptly by pointing to some birds pecking around a group of rocks a few yards away. "They're nice - what are they?"

"Wheatears. They like it around here."

Another long pause. Okay, I thought, if she wants to chat about birds. "You get some good sightings here at this time of year. We saw an American Blue Heron once. Blown hundreds of miles off course."

"Oh. Fascinating."

I'd had enough by then and shifted position to get up only for her to grab my elbow. "Sorry, didn't mean to be sarcastic. I never used to be like this. As for Gerald, well it could be dementia, who knows? The consultants diagnosed some form of PTSD, Post Traumatic Stress Disorder. Which isn't surprising considering the explosion."

Astonished, I blurted: "Explosion!? Sounds serious!"

"Yes, it was." She screwed up her nose, wiped something from her eye. A tear, a speck of grit, I couldn't discern. "Yes, profoundly serious. Two people dead, and our life wrecked. Not that it was ever anything to write home about, but... well, at least it was a life."

I struggled to respond. In the awkward silence, she climbed to her feet, waited for me to stand, then picked up her waterproof, slung it over her shoulder and moved away. A few yards down the path she stopped, turned, and called: "We'll be in the bar later. He still enjoys his beer."

*****

The island's hotel, decorated shabby chic with bits of boats, fishing nets and lobster pots, was busy. Mr and Mrs Wilson occupied a small corner table. I bought drinks, a pint for him, a double vodka and tonic for her - "Thank you, call me Helen."

"Okay, I'm Adam."

"No, you're not," Mr Wilson piped up. He leaned forward, nudging his glass and dislodging the froth from the top of his beer. "I know him," he said, prodding his wife's shoulder. "Trouble-maker." He drank quickly and loudly, smeared his mouth with his sleeve, sat back, and dozed off. A minute later his head lolled to one side and he jerked upwards, eyes wide and bewildered. "You're tired," she said. "Better get to bed before you start frightening people with your snoring."

Helping him from his chair wasn't easy although she curtly refused any support. "I'll be back in a few minutes. I'd like to finish my drink in peace." On her return she downed her glass in one. I bought her another with a slice of lime floating on the top. She picked it up daintily, squeezed it into her mouth, and dropped the arc of rind into the ashtray. Then she talked. "I tell everyone it's not his fault. But, actually, it is. He was the one who blew us all up."

Deadpan. She might have been talking about the rise in the cost of living rather than some catastrophic event.

"Oh, don't look at me like that," she said. "You think I'm cold, don't you? Well, maybe I am. But I have to navigate a way through it, day after day. I can't afford too much emotion. I just go through the practicalities."

She downed more vodka. Helen, the art teacher whom all the lads had fancied, was in her late 60s, still trim in her jeans and sweater. Celtic designed silverware dangled from her ears, heavy mascara muddied her eyelashes, and long, slender fingers, the tips varnished in azure, fiddled nervously with a cigarette lighter. There was a flick of ash-grey hair, another sudden gulp of alcohol, and then the hard-eyed challenge. I accepted it.

"So, what happened exactly?"

"What happened?" The lighter went skidding across the table. I pushed it back to her.

"Sorry. What happened? Gerald and his experiments, that's what happened. He had a shed, called it his garden laboratory. I warned him constantly about storing gas cylinders there, but he didn't listen and one day there was an almighty bang. Our house and next door's caught fire. We got out but our neighbour and her niece died. Lovely girl she was, studying dentistry.

"So unlucky. The girl, Sadie. Normally she would have been at college, but her train was cancelled so she'd nipped back to her aunt's to wait for the next one. What do they call that? Circumstantial luck? Isn't that what they teach in philosophy? External forces beyond your control, etcetera."

Helen sighed, sucked on a cigarette. "She had gorgeous hair, burnt umber, past her shoulders. Strange. Gerald didn't have a mark on his body but you could hardly say he was fortunate. It destroyed him. Couldn't accept that he was responsible, so he shut himself off. The psychiatrist said something about Disassociated Memory. And now? Well, you've seen him."

"What about you? Do you still do any art?"

She sniffed. "No, I told you. No time, no energy for it. It's full-on looking after him. Nobody realises. Put him in a home, they all say. Oh yes. So easy. But I can't. Just can't." Tears welled but she wiped them away, slowly, like a careful brush-stroke. "He was very clever, you know. And funny. Made me laugh.

And the thing is, while it's hard, I don't know what I'd do without him. It's my life and..."

A shout and a burst of laughter from a group of beach boys standing at the bar interrupted her. "Oh my God," she gasped. Twisting around, I saw Gerald, barefoot and in his candy-striped pyjamas, walking towards the exit. We managed to pull him back to their room where she murmured: "Goodbye," before closing the door.

Outside was pitch black. Another front was coming in, the wind freshening, rain in the air, but instead of the broad and safe concrete path, I opted for the scenic route back to our cottage. Heavy cloud switched off any light from the sky, but the episode with the Wilsons had left me at odds with myself. I needed to focus on something else, and the gale, sweeping in from the west, and the narrow, stony cliffside track offered a stern test of concentration.

Even so, as I skirted an outcrop with the waves slapping against the rocks 40 feet below, I stumbled over a rock, only just managing to regain my balance and avert a fatal fall by grabbing a branch of an old, stunted gorse bush. The thorns ripped my hand but I held on. I cursed my foolishness and was struck by another memory.

Mr Wilson screeching: "Collins, stop messing with the Bunsen. Do you want to blow us all up?"

How we all laughed.

*'The water covered outlying rocks, then mudflats,
and began to impinge on the sand, white for
most of the day but now alchemised into a
golden strand by the low October sun...'*

GOOD OLD MUM

(Entered for a crime fiction competition, max words 250 – a sweet little story of a Victorian era convict)

J AMES Devine sat on his plank bed, straight-backed against the limed wall, and tried to figure out when he was happiest. Not the moment he did the stupid bank clerk, three shots, blood spouting from his head and chest. Satisfaction, that was. But real happiness was when he handled the Colt 32 'Pocket' shooter for the first time. Tiny but lethal. The cool blue metal reflecting off his glasses. Pointing it at the mirror in his gaslit bedroom, squinting along the barrel, blasting the old Devine to Kingdom Come, lifting his head to welcome the new Devine. Murmured to himself: 'Now no-one will call you names.'

His reverie was broken by the rattle of the spyhole being opened and snapped shut. A warder shouting: "He's away with the fairies again. Bloody suicide watch – he can top himself for all I care." When next the door rattled, the warder entered carrying a tray. "Wake up Speccy Four Eyes, a last supper from your Mummy." A huge mutton pie.

She always said he needed feeding up. All skin and bone. Bit late now.

Devine poked around the dish with his wooden spoon, not hungry. Something hard at the bottom. He extricated the Colt, wiped gravy off with his hankie and inspected the chamber. Good old mum. One cartridge. For himself, obviously. Which showed she had never really understood him. Devine stuffed the revolver under the straw mattress, and smiled as he pictured the warder coming in again, making one of his sarcastic remarks.

Before his execution in 1901, James Devine made this sketch of his prison cell. Later, Irish Republican prisoners were held here.

MISS STOOPE'S DOUBLE CROSS STITCH

*(Entered into a competition for historical fiction
to include the prompt 'the middle ground', max
words 4,000 – a tale of the old American West)*

C UTTING from the Long Beach Press/
Telegram, August 6 1937:
*Cora D Stoope, who passed on Wednesday last
aged 80, was a popular and deeply respected citizen
of Long Beach best known for her close and lifelong
association with the Silver Princess and her wild
and woolly tales of 19th century outlaws rather than
the intricate needlework which attracted so many
clients, young and old, rich and poor to her tiny
dressmaking shop on Ocean East Boulevard. There,
she treadled away on her Singer or sat hand-stitching
on a hard ladder-backed chair. The finished product,
an extra panel in a sequined dress to accommodate
a lady's maturing figure, or new leather buttons on*

a woollen winter coat suitable for a holiday in the Rockies, was always precise and immaculate despite her deteriorating eyesight.

Her clientele included Hollywood actresses and the wives, widows and divorcees of affluent Californian businessmen who made fortunes in mining and oil during the Long Beach boom years. But she never exploited their wealth. One of her proud boasts – there were others – was that her fees were the same for the millionaires as for their servants. And, as a result, while she was constantly touched by wealth, she never got rich.

Her unfashionable premises remained a place of work, the floor strewn with loose cotton, balls of wool and fabric remnants. Electric lighting was too harsh, casting too many reflections, she would explain to a customer as, late on an autumn afternoon with the room darkening, she would light an oil lamp. Her rooms above the shop were simply furnished (although as no-one was ever invited upstairs the layout and facilities were a mystery until after her death) and, while she de-constructed and re-constructed beautiful items of clothing with meticulous care, her own apparel lacked colour and modernity, although, of course, it was always in impeccable repair.

It can be clearly observed that Cora D Stoope (no-one ever discovered what the D stood for) was a modest woman without airs and graces, content with the safe and unchallenging middle ground of life, where compromise deflects conflict and etiquette counts more than material gain. Clients were welcomed graciously, shown to a comfortable chair, and offered a cold drink, home-made lemonade in a tall glass or, when the winter gales were howling, a small cup of coffee. They understood why Cora made the ideal lady's companion and why Susan Bransford, The Silver Princess, held her in such high esteem.

Cora spoke quietly, patiently waiting her turn in any conversation, and rarely criticised anyone but herself, sometimes uttering 'Oh, you foolish girl,' after identifying a false stitch or forgetting where she had left a certain pair of scissors. However, in particular circumstances, she sometimes drifted back to earlier times with wonderful stories, related in the vernacular and designed to shock and entertain in equal measure, providing her audience with another side to 'Miss Stoope', the seamstress.

*****

CORA D Stoope was 15 and growing up fast when Jesse James aimed a Colt 45 at her and said through his thick, dark beard: "Close your eyes."

But she didn't. Or, rather, she couldn't. She stood rooted in the mud and mayhem of Main Street, Richmond, Missouri, scarcely able to breathe, her head ringing from the shouts, screams, pounding hooves and gunshots. Men dying.

Jesse laughed. "You're a purty young thing. Will make someone a fine wife." Holstered the gun, dug his stirrups into his horse's flanks and rode away.

'Take me with you,' she called, scaring herself for a moment in case she had said it aloud. But the only person near was young Bob Ford who stared wide-eyed and open-mouthed as America's most famous outlaw galloped imperiously down Main Street, Richmond and faded from view. If she had articulated her thoughts, then still he wouldn't have heard. Wouldn't have moved if a wagon train was thundering towards him.

Cora never did marry. Oh, she had chances. Notably, the aforesaid Robert Ford. But that was before he killed Jesse and became a celebrity. Or a notoriety, depending on your viewpoint.

"You knew Robert Ford – the Coward?" the folk of Long Beach would ask, struggling to reconcile this softly-spoken, elderly dressmaker with one of the West's most treacherous characters. Young Bob Ford. Shot Jesse in the back, spent the rest of his life posing and acting the fool - 'til someone gave him a dose of his own medicine.

"Yes, we grew up in the same street," she told them. "Ray County was full of outlaws and young men with wild ideas."

Cora had learned to judge which of her clients wanted it. Her story. Didn't even have to glance up from her Singer, just knew from the shuffle of feet, the scrape of the chair leg as they shifted position. Backwards, they'd heard enough, wanted their skirt or blouse or whatever it was she was mending and to get out. Forwards was a slightly different noise and implied interest. That's when she stopped treadling, brushed the trails of thread off her dress and inquired if they might take a coffee, even have a drop of something in it?

Outside, Ocean East Boulevard might be shimmering with light, heat hazy or windy but Cora's shop with its tiny shuttered window stayed dim, cool and calm. At least that's how it seemed – even In the earthquake of '21.

"And so, yes dear, pull the chair up. So you want to hear about Bob. Well, we went back a long, long way. You see…" This is where she paused, frowning slightly as though picking her words carefully even though she had them off pat, before folding her hands on her lap, gazing at them for a few seconds. When she looked up, she was ready.

"You see, Bob was there with me. When Jesse threatened to blow us both to Kingdom Come. You must have heard about it, the bank raid in Richmond. Three of our people killed. Typical of the James gang, they weren't that smart, y'know.

"Anyway, myself and Bob – we're just around the corner from the bank near the hitching rail, hearing all the commotion, wondering what on earth is going on, and then Jesse, he comes running out of the bank. There's a woman crying. Mayor Smith, he's sat on the sidewalk over the way and I think he should be doing something, then I see his shirt is all red.

"Anyhows, Jesse jumps on his mustang, sees us standing there, gawping. I mean, Jesse James. This big revolver in his hand and Bob on his knees blubbing and mumbling something like: 'Don't kill me. Please don't kill me.' And I'm thinking, what about me Bob? What about me? But Bob was like that. That's when I realised I didn't want to be wed to him although, I have to confess, it was some time before I actually turned him away."

Here, Cora might halt, allow her client time to fully digest that tragic, life-changing moment. To empathise.

"Had he asked you to marry him, Miss Stoope?"

"Oh yes. I was still young but we'd known each other forever. He was good-looking. I wasn't too bad myself." A demure glance from under her eyebrows. "Though you might not think so now," with a vague simper and a slight shift of her shoulders. Body language was so important, as she had told that Robert Mitchum only the other day.

The customer's response was usually immediate and forceful. "Miss Stoope, you do yourself an injustice. You've still got it." Which, to be fair, was what they said at the Players' Guild where she helped with the costumes. "My, Miss Stoope, you could have been in the movies." Even Mitchum, the Guild's rising star (though he still had much to learn about acting) complimented her in his rough-cast way of speaking. "Hey, Miss Stoope, like to jump a railcar with me?" He had ridden the boxcars across America, looked tough, but hadn't killed anyone. Why, not even John Dillinger could match old Jesse for toughness.

"Please, carry on." A distant voice pulling her from her reverie.

And so she did, her mid West accent coming

through more acutely the longer she talked, punctuated with increasingly theatrical gestures.

"Yes, thank you. Where was I – ah, outside the bank. Well, Jesse's away, a whoopin' and a hollerin' and Bob, he gets up, smacks the dust off his pants with his hat and says: 'Folk are not going to believe this. How we stood up to Jesse James.' And I said, no, they won't. But they did, some of them. And he revelled in it. Started packing a fancy handgun. Boasting. Said he was going to join the James Gang.

"I told him he wasn't up to it, he'd get himself killed but he was Robert Ford. Head in the clouds. He quit Richmond soon after, went looking for Jesse and his brother, Frank. Caused a lot of mischief. Held up a train once."

The almost casual way this information was imparted by a 70s something dressed in Victorian black always evoked an intake of breath.

"Good heavens, Miss Stoope. You sure had some interesting acquaintances! But Robert Ford, how come he changed so sudden from a scared baby pants to a vicious outlaw?"

Cora always had an answer, but never gave it away without a 'Hmm, that's a good question, I'll have to think about it for a second or two' sort of face. The frown, a fingertip to her forehead.

"Well, I never considered it like that. You have to understand what it was like in those days. Some getting rich too quick. Some staying forever poor. Boys running around wild. Give them a gun and in a split of a whisper they're transformed into a man, some kinda folk hero, having a poke at the Establishment.

They robbed the banks who wouldn't lend you money. They held up the trains that ran right across your land. At least that's how it was for a while. But the more righteous citizens, those with most to lose, got tired of it. It was affecting business so when Bob shot Jesse in the back, well he was a coward, but also a saviour."

"What did you think of him?"

"I was angry. He picked up a ten thousand bucks reward and didn't give me a dime." Here Cora would silently count up to five, ramping up the tension before dropping her bombshell.

"After all, I helped him plan it."

The reaction varied. 'My goodnesses', 'Good heavenses', and explosive 'Whats' aplenty. But some stared at her in utter bewilderment and one or two tried to disguise their embarrassment by taking a draught of coffee.

Had you ever heard the like? Cora D Stoope, grey-haired, hunched, and holding a magnifying glass to the eye of a needle, claiming involvement in one of America's most celebrated murders?

Gloria Davis, fingering the neatly altered hemline on her shift, told a friend over cocktails in Joe Jons' bar: "I nearly burst out laughing. There's this gentle old soul, still looks good but must be near 80, stitching up my dress and she's telling me the most dreadful things. All fiction, obviously. She could make a fortune with the studios as a script writer."

When Robert Mitchum walked in one day, asking for her advice – simply out of politeness - both on the cut of his clothes and about acting, Cora sat him down, said he looked okay, better than Cagney although she preferred Flynn, but if he wanted to make it big in L.A. he needed to work his body, his hands and face. Expression. Heck, she thought, Bob knew how to do it. Surrounded by flashing cameras, he'd pout, sneer, flaunt. And he could talk, too. Would have been a heart-throb in the silents.

 But Long Beach, affluent and sophisticated, was a different world than her dusty Ray County. Sometimes she leaned back from her Singer and eased out her saddest memory like unpicking a knotted thread. It moistened her eyes, even after 60 years, so she only did it occasionally, when no-one was around.

There was Bob, looking oh so fine and dandy. "I've come back Cora. Waddya think?"

One foot planted on the doorstep, his coat thrown open, revealing a pair of holstered six-shooters and a diamond studded waistcoat. But, by then, it was too late.

"Want me to take a picture, Bob?" she said, acid burning the words.

"Ah, come on Cora. It's me. I've made it. I've got the dough, we can go anywhere, do anything."

She sneered. "From what I've heard, Bob, you're a wastrel. Now get your dirty boot out of my door.

Coward!"

She heard him ride out. When news came through that he had been blasted to death by a nobody with a shotgun she blurted: "Live by the sword, die by it," and ran to her bedroom, leaving her parents speechless.

*****

Cutting from Salt Lake City Tribune, August 16, 1937:

Letter to the Editor

Dear Sir,

It is with deep regret that I must inform you that Miss Cora D Stoope died recently in Long Beach, Ca, where she had lived and worked since the end of the Great War. Cora will be remembered with deep affection by many in SLC.

She was the first cousin and most devoted friend of Susan Bransford Emery Holmes Delitch Egalitcheff, better known as the Silver Princess, one of the world's richest women and garlanded socialite. Both came from Richmond, Missouri, but spent long periods in SLC, particularly at my establishment, The Albany, where Susan kept our most luxurious suite.

These two ladies, so different in character, were inseparable. Susan invested heavily in several of my projects, including the Albany and the National Parks Highway, and Miss Stoope was always on hand to offer practical advice and support. Both now are gone from us and SLC and the wider world are the poorer for their absence.

Yours respectfully, Gus Holmes

*****

While Cora was revered by all those who entered her shop, she had no friends in Long Beach. In fact, she'd had only one true confidante in all her 80 years and even that relationship soured after the ghost had popped up. Even so, Susie was always with her, in spirit, though she might be flouncing through the lobby of Claridge's in London or the Hotel de Crillon in Paris, brushing off photographers, just at the moment Cora was smothering the oil lamp at the end of another humdrum day before toiling up squeaky stairs to her convent style room. An iron bedstead, a pine chest of drawers lovingly carved by her father, a wash-basin and a wooden cross hanging from a wall hook.

So different from earlier times when they travelled the breadth of America, though not the length as Susie was wary about bumping into certain ex Confederate characters in the south. At the end of each tour they finished up at the Albany where the proprietor Gus Holmes, a showman if ever there was, would be waiting at the colonnaded front entrance, hands out in greeting. Or supplication.

"Welcome home Princess," he'd gush, a diminutive balding man and a giant in Utah's mining, banks and hospitality industries. And, after kissing her lightly on each cheek, he would escort them to a table in the dining room with its 30 feet high ceiling and ornate plasterwork, summoning staff to fetch this and that until Susie leaned back, sighed and said: "So good to be back," or words to that effect and it was then and only then that Holmes might notice that Cora was also there. "And, Miss Stoope," - always Miss Stoope never Cora – "you're well, I hope?"

Of course, Cora always was well. How could she be otherwise? The poor cousin, lady in waiting to American royalty.

Susie, once a hairdresser, stood high in the Rich List thanks to two marriages into silver mining interests. First in line was Emery, second Holmes (no relation to Gus) with two more in the offing, a Serbian surgeon and an exiled Russian prince. Along the way she added their names to hers like trophies, indeed like the scalps she once saw looped around a Cheyenne warrior's lance, so that in time she became Susan Bransford Emery Holmes Delitch Englalitcheff. But at the height of her fame and influence, in America's Gilded Age, she was usually referred to as The Silver Princess, a tall, elegant if hard-boned woman, who roamed the world's finest hotels and restaurants catching the eye of noblemen and Press barons.

Cora and Susie were ensconced at the Albany in the autumn of 1901 when a masculine apparition invaded the sanctity of the ladies' waiting room. Not one immediately recognisable, and not one likely to impress, scare or enchant. A bamboo walking stick to combat arthritis and thinning white hair straggling beyond his neck and ears.

Pegging his way over to their sofa, he sat down heavily and said: "Well, after all these years. Cora Stoope, I'll be darned. I never forget a face."

"Well," said Cora, primly. "I've obviously forgotten yours."

"Understandably," he replied in a peculiar high-pitched voice which made Cora recoil. "But I bet you one silver dollar you remember the last time we looked into each other's eyes." He sniggered, wiping spittle from his lips with the back of his hand. "Yes lady. I sure bet you do."

Cora scoured his face, gasped and clutched Susie's hand. Susie carefully withdrew it. She didn't relish people getting too close, physically nor emotionally, although she had always had a care for her cousin, po-faced maybe, but loyal and devoted as any good plantation slave.

But that momentary contact had enabled Cora to settle. She sniffed dismissively (a mannerism cultivated from the Princess).

"So, Susie," she said with a hint of stage-managed superiority. "Seems to me we've got another imposter on our hands. Another gold digger."

Susie looked hard at her. "But who is he imposting, Cora? Who? I'm in the dark here, and I don't much care for it."

Cora's chin lifted. "Hmm – I wonder who?"

The man grimaced, bent forward, offered his hand to Susie: "Jesse James, charmed to meet you."

"Susan Emery Holmes Bransford" (her third and fourth husbands were still over the horizon). "And

I'm not so charmed to meet you. Whoever you might turn out to be. I'll leave you in Cora's capable care." With that she stood, eschewed the attention of two staff who were charged with monitoring her every move, and strode as only the Silver Princess could stride, towards the lift.

"I've read much about her," said Jesse. If, of course, he was Jesse. Cora had dealt with several fakes over the years, Abe Lincoln, Billy the Kid, George Custer all alleging they had never died in the first place, that they had been part of complex conspiracies. All pan-handling for Susie's money. Now the most brazen of all. America's most murderous outlaw. Gunned down by Cora's childhood sweetheart, young Bob Ford. Long ago.

"Take your shirt off," Cora ordered. "Show me."

And he did. Right there, in the quiet, luxurious ladies waiting room of Salt Lake City's flagship hotel. Laid down his thick woollen jacket, pulled off his necktie, shrugged off the linen shirt, lifted his vest. He understood perfectly. And while a group of ladies in one corner, and a solitary Miss in another, muttered and gawped, Cora inspected his torso, first the front, then the back.

"My, my. You certainly took your fair share of lead. So, where you been sneaking off to all this time?"

Jesse, for it was he, did not answer until dressed, grinning all the while at the room. This time he chose a chair opposite Cora, lit a cigar, wondered if she would call for a whiskey, and waited. When the drink arrived, he downed it in one and recited the truth. "The truth Cora, not what the world was told."

"See," he went on. "I reckon I've paid my debt to society. Thirty years or so of keeping low, bridling my mouth, hiding my face. Living on Dirt Street. I'm here to recoup something of what I'm owed."

Which Cora appreciated, having realised as soon as she had seen the bullet scars, all in the right places, that Jesse James had unfinished business with her.

"You really shouldn't have trusted young Bob," he said. "It's not easy to shoot a man. Even in the back. And if you hesitate, well, you'll be the one lying in the dust with your lifeblood seeping away."

"Maybe I should have done it myself."

"Maybe you should. Fact is Cora, Bob never got to pull his gun. He told me all about it, your plan. At first I thought to kill him, then come looking for you. But, there was some merit in it. I'd had enough of all the warring by then. Best way to end it, try to start a new life, was to die. Now I'm not so sure, but too late now."

Always a good talker, weren't you Jesse, thought Cora as his voice rose and fell, distant then close. She recalled the day when, two years after the Richmond robbery, Bob Ford told her he'd joined up with the James Gang. Did she want to meet them?

They rode out to the Wilsons' ramshackle farm just over the border into Kansas. Jesse was reticent, skulking on the porch, hat tilted over his eyes, boots hooked onto the rail. Hardly the dashing Robin Hood of the Wild West, that some figured him. But as the sun dipped he took her into the weed strewn garden with his young son and they sat and watched while he dug for worms. He had a thing about worms. Then they went fishing.

"How many times you been shot?" she asked him.

Jesse laid down his rod, hauled his shirt off his shoulders. "See for yourself."

Three marks of note, shoulders and chest. "And one that I can't show you," he said. If he expected her to blush, he was mistaken.

"Would you have shot me that time? Outside the bank."

Jesse turned, asked: "Did I tell you to close your eyes?" She nodded. "Well then," he said and went back to casting his line over the water.

In the ladies waiting room of the Albany Hotel, Salt Lake City, Jesse was finishing his story. One of cold-blooded murder, lies and deceits, unsuitable for the hearing of real ladies. As Jesse's unpalatable voice squeaked on, Cora glanced around the room. No-one else in it now, the other women sensing discord and retreating into the protective depths of the hotel.

Susie viewed the Albany as home. Not a second home, just home. Whereas Cora quickly grew weary of its soft padded seats, deep mattresses and professional insouciance and excused herself as soon as possible to return to Richmond. Now, despite its thick Wilton carpet and heavy French furniture, the room contained only Jesse's whine, mincing the air with its intrinsic malevolence.

"See Cora, the way it happened…"

"Easy to guess," she interrupted fiercely. "I imagine they did you a deal. Buried someone else, you providing the body of some unfortunate, and let you go as long as you stayed out of trouble and stopped writing to the newspapers about all the corrupt politicians. That's how I see it, Jesse."

He glared at her. "Maybe. Of course Bob pledged to share the ten thousand but, well, he reneged." That old steel glinting. "So, without wishing to impose too much more, I'm here to collect."

Cora stiffened. In as much as her corset and well starched, heavily brocaded gown would allow.

"I never got any of the money. Bob went off, east. Playing in theatricals, buying saloons. New York. Then he was in Utah and Colorado. Where he got his dues."

Jesse stroked his beard. An old habit as though coaxing secrets or worms from it.

"Point is Cora Stoope. Whether Bob or you. I'm owed. And Bob's dead. You can get the money, the Silver Princess has got millions. She won't miss ten grand."

He rose slowly grunting with pain. "You bring it. Tomorrow. Five o'clock in the afternoon. At the corner of the Great Tabernacle and South Drive. You hear me.

"And don't bother telling tales to anyone. You say that Jesse James is out on the street and they'll look at you kinda sideways and think you've missed your medicine. Because everyone knows I'm dead and buried, all official and well documented."

Jesse was having trouble standing upright. He leaned on the back of the chair, looked down at her. "Seems to me Cora, that we've both been living a life full of compromise. Me, to escape gaol. Maybe the gallows. But you – I don't get it. You've chosen it, stuck in this middle ground like you've walked into a swamp and allowed it to suck all the imagination and ambition out of you. I despise that."

Her head dipped and for a second or two he felt a new sadness.

"See here, I've not come to lecture you. I just want what's owed me. And remember this,   I've looked people in the face and killed them. And I'll do it again come the time."

But, recovered from her moment of weakness, Cora returned his gaze, noted again his once powerful now scrawny frame, his misty eyes, and his trembling right hand.

"How old are you?, Jesse? Let me think, nearing 60 I shouldn't wonder. And looking a few years beyond that, if I might be so bold."

Jesse sneered. "Tomorrow, Five in the afternoon." Trying to swivel, he lost his balance slightly, recovered and walked out, his stick silently prodding the carpet.

As she expected Susie refused to believe her, accused her of fantasising, of concocting some ridiculous myth to induce her to part with her money, even with conspiring with a felon masquerading as Jesse. A terrible scene ensued. Long-held grievances aired, bitterness searing through the hotel's soft-scented atmosphere, and, while they were eventually reconciled the relationship was forever tinged by the truths spat out in anger and disappointment, but truths all the same.

Next day, Cora met Jesse under the overhang of the Great Tabernacle where they might be perceived as sheltering from the rain.

"If you think I've got any money for you you're wrong."

Jesse pointed at a small bag in her left hand. "So what's that in there?"

She unclipped it. Pulled out a Colt revolver, a small pocket weapon designed for women and travellers yet her hand was hardly big enough to wrap around the butt. Steady enough, though. And point-blank range, the barrel only inches from his belly, threatening him with another bullet hole.

"Must admit you've got more guts than Bob. Wouldn't like to bet against you pulling that trigger."

Trying to bluff through a crisis. Typical Jesse.

"Close your eyes."

He did but smiled. "Like I said before, it's not easy to pull the trigger, Is it Cora?"

Click. A misfire. She reached out to steady him as his knees buckled. Smelled something unpleasant.

"Huh, your lucky day, Jesse or whatever name you go by now."

The ghost limped away without a word his stick tapping an uncertain rhythm on the sidewalk.

*****

Cutting from the Richmond Times, April 7, 1962:

A series of personal scrapbooks, highlighting life in Richmond in the late 19th century, has been unearthed during a recent furniture auction in Long Beach, Ca. They were discovered in a secret drawer of a chest once owned by Miss Cora D Stoope, whose family lived in Richmond 1840-1914 and whose house still stands.

Miss Stoope who died in Long Beach in 1937 aged 80 was a dressmaker to the rich and famous of the West Coast including several Hollywood stars, notably Robert Mitchum. She took to the stage herself occasionally with the Guild of Players in Long Beach and regularly submitted gangster and Western movie scenarios to MGM, Universal and other studios under the pseudonym of Cora Ford.

One of her screenplays, cryptically entitled 'Stitched Up', has also come to light and is being considered by production agents in L.A.

However her scrapbooks mostly reflect the quieter, more conservative society of Missouri and the Richmond Times have been granted permission to feature some of them on an occasional basis.

We begin today with her fond memories of a day's fishing with her Uncle Jesse.

Main Street, Richmond, Missouri – in the days when Cora D Stoope bumped into Jesse James (or said she did..)

UNCLE FRED'S PIE

*(Essay published in History UK Magazine –
how one man helped Britain survive WW2)*

BRITAIN faced two great threats in the early stages of WW2 – bombs and starvation. Courage and unbending spirit helped the nation to survive the Blitz and one man' s superb business efficiency stemmed the pangs of hunger.

Lord Woolton, the Minister for Food, was determined that Britain's larder remained well stocked, and that, despite rationing and poverty, everyone had something to put on the table.

"We must all be fighting fit," he declared.

Yet through the hellish winter of 1940-41 when the bombs rained down on major cities and ports, Britain was perilously close to running out of grub. Traditionally, two thirds of its food was imported but the war had devastated supply routes and even when ships did survive the Atlantic crossing there were difficulties unloading their cargoes because of bomb damage.

Woolton, a scientist turned businessman turned civil servant, launched the National Food Campaign urging people to make weaker tea ('one for you, one for me and none for the pot' saved 50 shiploads of tea a year) and never to peel potatoes.

Betty Driver, the singer who became the Coronation St character Betty Turpin, regaled radio audiences with a popular ditty:

> *Those who have the will to win,*
> *cook potatoes in their skin*
> *knowing that the sight of peelings*
> *deeply hurts Lord Woolton's feelings.*

Formerly chair of the John Lewis Company, Woolton was a superb team leader and quickly had the Ministry of Food working at full tilt particularly on propaganda. Soon Britain was awash with posters proclaiming 'Waste Not, Want Not', 'Grow Your Own' and 'Eat Up Your Greens'. Brief adverts known as food flashes popped up on cinema screens and cartoon characters like 'Doctor Carrot' and 'Potato Pete' appeared in newspapers and magazines.

He even promoted a story that eating carrots improved the sight of Britain's successful night time fighter pilots.

Perhaps the most influential marketing ploy was a radio programme broadcast six days a week after the morning news aimed primarily at housewives and entitled 'The Kitchen Front' in which well-known cooks offered advice and cheap but sustaining recipes. One was Woolton Pie, a veg mixture thickened with oatmeal and topped with pastry.

With meat and eggs severely rationed and citrus fruits rarely available, Woolton was aware that people needed more than veg. Children and the poor were particularly vulnerable. His solution was free school meals and milk for 650,000 youngsters and the 'British Restaurant' a nationwide scheme of basic cafes often run by volunteers and where, for eight pennies, you could tuck into a plate of meat and veg with bread and a pudding.

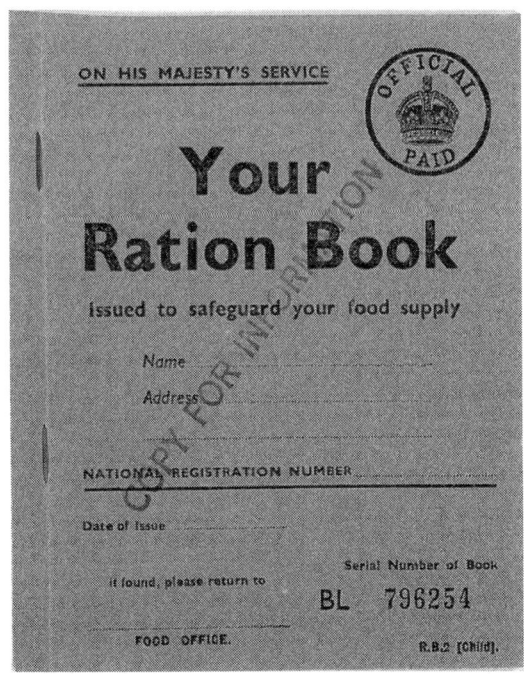

Woolton, who was born Frederick Marquis and brought up in the terraced streets of Salford and Manchester, had a natural affinity with the working class and, after graduating from Manchester University, he lived in an impoverished district of Liverpool carrying out social work. One day a woman neighbour was found dead in her home – she had starved to death. The tragedy informed Woolton for the rest of his life.

When he moved into business and later into the highest ranks of the civil service he also moved easily within the circles of the nation's wheeler-dealers, major industrialists and top politicians and by the time he was drafted into the wartime effort he had a deep knowledge of how Britain worked.

Despite that, his initiatives would not have succeeded had he lacked communications skills and charisma. The tall grey-haired Woolton, impeccably dressed, stood out in any company. He talked easily and persuasively both in War Cabinet conferences and on the radio where he made countless broadcasts and became affectionately known to listeners as 'Uncle Fred'.

Of his few critics Winston Churchill was one especially when Woolton organised a lunch for him, and the new USA ambassador. The venue was London's Savoy Hotel where the chef was usually tasked with producing an exotic recipe like crayfish with foie gras but on this occasion had been ordered to put a Woolton Pie on the table. The surprised and disgruntled PM demanded a plate of cold beef instead and afterwards complained bitterly only for Woolton to stand his ground, insisting that rich and poor had to tighten their belts.

Gradually Churchill was won over and Woolton given his head. He limited restaurant meals to three courses with a maximum price of five shillings, introduced the national loaf (a nutritious but unpopular wholemeal bread) and threatened anyone who wasted food with a possible two years prison term or a £500 fine, a measure aimed at the profiteers rather than normal households. And powdered milk was made available to some of the country's key workers – vermin hunting cats used to protect food stacked in warehouses.

Thankfully from May 1941 the USA shipped over cargoes of eggs, flour, cheese, lard and canned milk. But without Uncle Fred's pie - a blend of organisation and efficiency under a thick crust of ingenuity - Britain would have struggled to survive.

Woolton went on to become Minister of Reconstruction, planning for Britain's future after the war and Chairman of the Conservative Party 1946-55. He died in 1964.

Lord Woolton

A ROUGH GUIDE TO SLATES

*(Written for a flash fiction competition
and commemorating the Scottish slate
industry – max words 250)*

ANDY isn't impressed by our garden decoration. "Old roof slates – what do you see in 'em?"

They hang from the rickety fence like a line of forlorn washing. Shades of grey/green with hints of ferrous red. With ridges, arches and whorls like fingerprints. Each unique, displaying its peculiar hues in different light.

"What do I see? History. And character."

Once they crowned homes and mills. Some date back 200 years, grabbed from the earth by quarrymen wielding iron bars, split with lump hammers and chisels, dressed with slate knives to the required shape. Then carefully laid in diminishing courses, biggest at the bottom, smallest at the top, creating centuries of protection. And an artwork.

In full production, the slate quarries 'roofed the world'. But they have been quiet for decades.

"You're a romantic," snorts Andy. "One thing – they're too heavy for that fence. Second – they could use a dab of paint, liven 'em up."

But why camouflage them? They're an archive. Stories. Images.

Of weather-beaten brows and tough, calloused hands.

Of faith. Believing the work would stretch forever with so much of the stuff waiting patiently to be uncovered and used.

Of broken promises.

The other night, in a strange dream, I saw our slates transform into twisted gargoyle-like faces. Anger, yes. But something else. Something odd...

Andy listens politely to all this. Still not convinced, he suddenly points: "Your fence is going over!"

He's right. So that's what it was. They were laughing.

VOICELESS

(Entered in a crime fiction competition, max words 3,500 - based on the facts of two books previously written by the author 'No Pity' and 'The Knutsford Suffragists')

E MILY CROMPTON, wife of a censorious stockbroker and daughter of a dog-collared disciplinarian, could not scream. Just wasn't in her blood. Neither could she slouch, not after a year at finishing school in Geneva. She sat bolt upright in her velvet covered chair, her arms dangling helplessly over the sides, mouth sagging open, and, although her vocal chords twitched, she was mute. The hall clock ticked. The horror continued unabated.

"And Ma'am, after that wicked man tried to have his way with me..."

Mary Jane Parsons sniffed, dabbed at her nose, refocused her gaze and realised that her mistress was staring wide-eyed at her, paying her genuine attention for the first time in the three years she had worked at Springwood House.

"And then? What?!" A furnace blast, much fiercer than Mrs Crompton intended. Her housemaid shuddered.

"Well, that's when I tripped over the body."

Mrs Crompton gasped and choked.

"Good heavens," she spluttered, recovering her voice if not her poise. "It's terrible, terrible. A scandal. What in heavens will we do?"

Mary Jane wondered how to respond. Years of servility in big houses came to her aid. "Should I ask cook to bring you some tea?" she asked meekly. But, an ugly thought suddenly reared its head. Scandal. Ah, well, girl, that's you on the rubbish heap.

Usually Mary Jane had great difficulty in making people listen. More than most, domestic servants appreciated the Suffragettes' call for 'Deeds Not Words' but not in the way Emmeline Pankhurst intended.

"Makes you laugh, doesn't it?" she once told the cook Winnie Pickstock after a Votes For Women rally on the nearby Common, placards high, artistic banners waving in the breeze. "Work our fingers to the bone, don't we? And not allowed to speak. We could tell them all about deeds not words."

"Yes," said Winnie, rolling out the pastry, "and they're not even fighting for the likes of us."

Communicating with Mrs Crompton often proved difficult. Mary Jane might say, as an extreme example: "Can you smell gas?" and Ma'am would continue to murmur sweet nothings to her Persian cat, Alexander, or to sweep the mantelpiece with her forefinger, checking it had been dusted properly. But now, with the noise of scandal filling the room, she had little choice but to pay heed.

She sipped the soothing Darjeeling, Lipton's Best, looking warily over the rim of her cup, Mary Jane still standing, bedraggled, soaking wet, clutching at her coat buttons, one of which was missing, another hanging loosely. And something on her sleeve? "Oh dear, that's blood, Ma'am."

Mrs Crompton's cup rattled in its saucer. Winnie relieved her of it, waited at her side. Their employer shifted position, tried to stand up, failed, and uttered a long drawn-out moan as she slipped back onto the chair, closed her eyes and surrendered.

"So, Mary Jane. I suppose you must tell me all of it."

Which she did in her light Welsh accent. And repeated to Sergeant William Prentice, in charge of the Lilyford Constabulary, and to me (with some embellishments after a couple of brandy and sodas). 'Big Bill' fancied himself as a high-flying detective while I daydreamed about a glittering newspaper career under the bright lights of the capital, far away from my deeply conservative, wrapped in cotton wool home town. We both salivated at the sheer potential of Mary Jane's misery.

Newspapers in Edwardian Britain gorged on tales of brutal death and this one made headlines throughout Britain.

Taking a Sunday evening stroll along Heathy Lane, the walls of a country estate on one side, rolling farmland on the other, rain starting to fall, Mary Jane was passed by a man on horseback, a man she recognised as George Ross, a wealthy local businessman, recently married with political aspirations and leading the region's Anti-Women's Suffrage League campaign. Ross dismounted, stopped her. He stank of alcohol. As she tried to manoeuvre past him, he dragged her through a field gate and was tugging at her clothes when disturbed by the sound of rapid fire gunshots, Crack! Crack! Crack! ripping the air. Ross leaped back into the saddle and galloped off.

"Like he was in the Derby," Mary Jane told Sergeant Prentice.

"You can tell she likes going to the music hall," he told me 'off the record'. "She's a bit of an actress, but I believe her. Let's face it, you couldn't make up a story like hers." He looked at me. "Although maybe you could." He wasn't joking.

Prentice had it all written down in indelible pencil on blue, lined notepaper. With her constant interventions, it had taken over two hours but, eventually, she signed it as a true and accurate account of her nightmare.

Distressed, bewildered, and with the hoofbeats of Ross's mount fading into the distance, she tottered back along the lane towards the town and safety, splashing through the puddles on the cinder track until, rounding a bend, she stumbled over a man lying on the verge, arms splayed out wide, his head entangled in the hedge. 'A crown of thorns,' she thought. For a second, she hoped he was merely drunk but touched his chest, saw his eyes staring into the murky sky, unblinking as raindrops splashed off his forehead. She stood there, uncomprehending, the rain hammering down, a body at her size three feet.   Suddenly, another figure emerged. From nowhere, it seemed, but probably from behind a nearby clump of hazel and alder trees. He looked hard at her, pulled something from his raincoat pocket, pointed it, put it back. Smiled, turned and walked away, enfolded by the gloom. Mary Jane's fingers were red and sticky. She wiped them on her sleeve.

 Violent death and sex – the simple facts were lurid enough but my editor ordered more local 'colour'. "You're born and bred here – use your contacts." Mrs Cunnellon, one of the more approachable tea-room gossips helped. "Bit of a show-off isn't she? Flouncing down the street, that tight skirt, no corset, flashing her ankles, head in the air as though she's a somebody rather than a maid. Don't know why Mrs Crompton puts up with it."

"And," her friend, Mrs Gunnery elaborated, "she's been seen dilly-dallying on the corner of Ladies' Lane. At night – and you know what that means." Yes. Even a small, affluent town like Lilyford had its seamier nooks and crannies, of which this particular tea-room was one, darkened by its hypocrisy, soured by antipathy. And cherished by guttersnipe scribes like yours truly.

As for Big Bill Prentice, he put down his copy of The Hound of the Baskervilles, muttering 'The world's greatest detective, my backside', and solved the murder without any help from Sherlock Holmes. John Bell, an Irish tailor lodging in the town, had been assassinated for no apparent reason other than proclaiming his support for independence. He had forgotten, perhaps, that Lilyford was a hotbed of Imperial patriotism which had provided a score of Volunteers for the Boer Wars – it would have been more but several badly nourished specimens were rejected as unfit for service, highlighting the fact that 25 per cent of our thriving, powerful country went hungry.

Helped by Mary Jane's description, vague though it was, Prentice quickly collared the shooter, a 21 years-old draper's son, a member of the Rifle Club, and recent purchaser of a powerful pocket pistol from Colt's mail order office in Pall Mall, London. ('Never fear a tramp' said their advert in Field and Gun). James Mallory was well-known and popular. His arrest caused outrage. Protestors gathered around the police station. No-one cared about the death of an Irish rebel although Bell was a clean-living, law-abiding man. But, if convicted, Mallory faced the hangman. No two ways about it. "He's just a kid," his Uncle Alf said. "Wouldn't hurt a fly." Yes, but I was acquainted with Mallory. Had seen him on the shooting range with an old service revolver, missing wildly from the normal position but advancing closer and closer until almost at point-blank range and then whooping in delight at hitting the bulls-eye. To his credit, Prentice stood his ground, affirming: "We have a witness who has identified him. All she has to do is confirm her story in the witness box." And he reassured her: "Don't worry. Just be guided by your conscience and we will have justice for Mr Bell."

All very well, retorted Mary Jane Parsons (to herself, of course, as housemaids were not allowed to voice grievances about anything; working conditions, wages, sexual assaults, for fear of being flung into the street and left to rot). But will there be justice for me?

No, Mary Jane. Not you or for any of your ilk.

*****

Allow me to spin the clock forward a few years to the winter of 1909 when I am coughing my way through the streets of the capital, the epicentre of a glorious, decadent Empire. Now on the books of an international news agency I'm on the trail of the Suffragettes, who have stepped up the militancy in their battle for women to have the vote. Not all women, though. Only respectable, middle-class ladies. Not women like Mary Jane Parsons. Why bring her into it again? Because she's here. Working the streets. And spitting at me when I offer help. "You never helped me afore. Why now?" She has a point.

Mallory's escape from the death sentence was

inevitable. Oh, he did it, for sure, we all knew that but questions about his mental stability vanished because, at the trial, he conducted himself properly while Mary Jane, flustered and under intense pressure from rows of hostile male eyes, appeared doubtful and confused. And her story of being assaulted by a gentleman on horseback produced sneers in the jury box and blatant laughter in the public gallery. The trial collapsed. Mallory was carried shoulder high from the court. Ross, exonerated, confronted her, sneering: "Liar. You're ruined now."

When I asked her for a comment, she sobbed: "They have no right to treat me like this, No right." I put my hand on her shoulder, but she brushed it off. "I'll have you know that in my time I've served countesses and earls and some of the things you've written about me are shameful. Just rumours and gossip. Shameful!" She turned and shuffled away, head bowed as usual. I could hardly say it was all about 'colour'. I shrugged and went to find Mallory who had promised me an exclusive interview.

But now in the chilly December of 1909, Mary Jane and I are in a Temperance Society coffee house on the north side of the river. She's famished but tries hard not to show it, nibbling at the cake I've bought her, but then biting into it ferociously. Crumbs stick to her lips. Other customers watch, some suspicious, others amused, wondering what she'll offer me in return for her iced bun. It is not a chance meeting. I searched for several weeks after a fellow newshound had written a teasing little story about a 'woman of the night' who had appeared in court for soliciting and had told the Bench that, while she had fallen low, she had once 'served countesses and earls'. Name of Mary Jane Crompton, the address a large, squalid boarding house amid the city's slums, where I hung around, asking questions and receiving few answers, except invitations to have a good time for a few shillings. Then, one autumn morning, I overheard an argument in the doorway, one woman demanding rent money, and a Welsh accent arguing for more time to pay. Mary Jane didn't recognise me immediately, but all I had to say was: "Remember Lilyford?" and her jaw dropped. I threw some cash at her landlady, took her by the elbow and steered her away. And here we sit, quiet and wary, until she finishes her cake, and I, not wanting food nor a 'good time', but only to hear her speak. Hear her.

The lilt of her voice, fashioned on a poor farm in Montgomeryshire, rises and falls like major and minor chords.

"I could understand some of it. Mrs Crompton, well she had a reputation to keep. Why did I use her name? Oh, just the spur of the moment when the bobbies arrested me. I didn't want to give my real one. I'd already dragged the family name through the mud, so Dada said." Pause to reflect. I wait, sipping lukewarm coffee. "No, they didn't want me back at home. Mam had passed, and he'd always preferred the boys to me. And, of course, without a character from the mistress, I had no hope of another place."

A pause while she carefully brushes crumbs off her sleeves and realise suddenly it's the same jacket she had all those years back, although all the buttons are in place and there is no hint of blood. She notices me staring, gives me a hard look, continues.

"I had a friend, Jessie, and she suggested we come to the capital. Bound to be work, she said. Lord knows what's happened to her. Anyway, we didn't find work, not regular. I don't have to tell you the rest." She stiffens a forefinger against her forehead. "Look at me. What do you see? Go on, tell me. I'm too scared to look in the mirror. On second thoughts don't tell me what you see." So I refrain. Where I might drag up the memory of a pretty, diminutive maid, others will view her only as a thin, shrunken prostitute with broken teeth and smeared lipstick. Gripping her cup of hot chocolate with both hands, she gazes out of the smudged window. The city is grey with rain and soot, the coffee house humid. Several women are among the customers, one young and fresh-faced, an office 'girl' perhaps, sitting by herself. Relaxed and confident. Times are changing. The Suffragettes are smashing windows. Perhaps Mary Jane reads my thoughts.

"There was a demonstration the other day," she says, as though I don't already know. "Women stamping up and down with banners. Purple for dignity, white for purity, and green for hope. That's me all over, isn't it?!" What might be a laugh sticks in her throat. Her chin tilts, a habitual pose, suggesting a certain conceit.

"Votes for Women. Strange. What we really need, women like me, are megaphones. To make people listen. Because, no-one does.'" Angry now. I saw her mood swings during the murder investigation, but nothing like this. "No-one. Not Mrs Crompton, not anyone in that accursed town, not the jury, not you. You're just like the rest. Indeed, you're worse!" Suddenly she sweeps her cup and plate off the table. They shatter on the tiled floor. The office girl scrapes back her chair, alarmed. Mary Jane is on her feet, her head haughtily thrown back, swearing she has always told the truth, and that one day everyone will hear and believe her. Seconds later she is gone, the door banging in her wake. When I inquire at the boarding house, they claim she has left, they know not where.

Twelve months later the Suffragettes launched a major protest outside Parliament. With the kind permission of the government, police used strong-arm methods to break it up. Among those arrested was a Mary Jane Parsons and, although she claimed that while being shoved into a Black Maria one constable had 'messed' with her, she was sentenced to three months in prison.

"Mary Jane is a hero," said Annie Kenney, Christabel Pankhurst's first lieutenant, having agreed to meet me at the Suffragettes' HQ, the Women's Social and Political Union office. "She is ready to die for the cause."

"Sounds like a good headline?" I said, provocatively. Kenney shook her head.

"Cynical as ever." We knew each other from the early days of Suffragism when she and Christabel visited Lilyford shouting their slogans from a platform on the Common - before they realised that words had little effect.

"But I always felt you were sympathetic to our cause. Maybe I was wrong." I let it go. I didn't want an argument, at least not before I had wormed more detail from her. For example, how a 'domestic' turned low-grade whore had become involved with the middle-class ranks of the Suffragettes. I reckoned Kenney, whose roots lay in the mill towns of the North, would rise to that.

"We're fighting for all women," she blazed. "If it hadn't been for us, Mary Jane would have died alone in a stinking back street." Apparently, a group of activists, on their way to a Christmas Day rally, had found her collapsed, half-starved and stained by urine, in a shop doorway. "They brought her here, and we nursed her back to health. Then she enrolled."

"Nursed her or indoctrinated her," I said, sourly. Kenney slapped her pencil down. "No. She put her name down willingly. You should have seen it, her face all lit up. A wonderful moment, like a baptism. And she has played her part." I wondered about

that. Planting explosives? Firing cricket pavilions?
 On her release in March 1911, I loitered outside
the women's gaol but was prevented from reaching
her by a posse of supporters. "She's in a bad way,"
said one, shoving me in the chest. There were
exclamations of disgust, and a shriek of "Good
God, what have they done to you?!" A tiny bundle,
wrapped in a cloak and a WSPU flag, was carried
into a waiting cab and borne away. She never
fully recovered from the ordeal, although it was
much later, when I returned from duty as a war
correspondent in France, that I learned of her fate.
A coat and a bag left on the river bank, and a
scrawled note, addressed to me, 'Mr Adams, The
Reporter'. The agency chief, grimacing, handed it
to me. It said: 'No vote, no voice. Remember me.'
Her bloated body had washed up a couple of miles
downstream, to be dumped into a paupers' grave, a
hero no more, just another victim.
 By then George Ross was richer than ever, thanks
to investment in Army boots and other military
equipment. Having moved south, he was living
in a luxurious apartment, overlooking one of the
capital's parks.
"Remember Mary Jane," I asked him, after
inveigling my way into his home on the pretext of
writing an admiring piece on his firm's war effort.
"No," he said, tapping his cigar into an ashtray. "I
think you'd better be off."
I shouted. "It's time you admitted what you did
to her. It destroyed her," throwing the note at

him. "Her epitaph!" He read it carefully, screwed it up, and burned it in the ashtray dousing the flame with a drop of his whisky. "Any further harassment," he said with the calm of a man of influence, "and I'll have to speak to my old friend Bill Prentice. He's a Detective Inspector at Scotland Yard now. I'll be seeing him at the next Lodge meeting."

*****

In the first summer of the peace I went back to Lilyford. Everyone involved had left long ago but Heathy Lane was unchanged. One Sunday evening I limped along it (a wartime bullet in my left knee was proving restrictive) and came to the field gate where Mary Jane's life had suddenly careered out of control. I tried to imagine her desperate struggle with Ross, and the air-splitting gunfire, but all I could see was a field of golden wheat and all I could hear was the breeze rustling through the hedgerows and trees.

*Annie Kenney and Christabel Pankhurst
demonstrating on the common close
to Springwood House.*

THE DIRT

*(Entered in an Edinburgh Arts Trust
competition, max words 2,000 – a candidate
in the 'gritty realism' category)*

J OHN DANIEL carried out his first bank raid on
October 12, 1973, a day before his 18th
birthday. He used a sawn-off shotgun hidden
in a rolled-up umbrella, a demand note carefully
printed in bold capitals by his mother, one of the
new-type plastic shopping bags and a trolley full of
bravado.

Daniel was five feet six inches tall in his Cuban
heeled boots and wore thick horn-rimmed specs,
an orange shirt and a black PVC coat. Carefully
positioning the brolly on the counter, he pushed
his mum's message at the cashier. She read it,
smiled, and handed it back. "Didn't know it was
Rag Week." Helen Murray, recently married, was
then five seconds from being blown to Kingdom
Come. Daniel wiggled the brolly so that the
twin barrels nosed through the end of it. His
finger creased the trigger, his mouth curled in
anticipation. Helen suddenly realised, stifled a

scream and handed over almost £3000. As he nonchalantly strolled out, she vomited violently and forgot to press the alarm.

Still a novice and far too cocky, Daniel was grabbed by police after drunkenly flashing money around at a night club. But there were obvious flaws in the prosecution case. Helen had described him as 'average height'. Yet, at his trial, Daniel could barely see over the lip of the dock having swapped his heels for flat slip-ons. And, as he told the jury he had never in his worst nightmare worn horn-rimmed specs, an orange shirt and a black PVC coat. "Not my style," he said. with his wide-faced charm and a flop of thick, black hair veiling his acned forehead. "Not my style at all," pinching the wide lapels of his pinstriped suit. From Burton's, £30 off the peg, the bulk of his earnings being nursed by his mother Jackie and girlfriend Sassy.

Daniel walked. Thanked the jury. Nodded to us in the Press Box. Jackie was waiting for him in the Crown Court's cobbled forecourt. Taking her arm, they ambled over to a green Vauxhall Estate, Sassy at the wheel, wishing it was a Triumph Stag or a Beemer Series 3, anything but this shed on wheels. "No showing off," Daniel had ordered, learning from his experience. She turned to him, bright-eyed, yellowing teeth. "Wow, I knew you were cool but the show you put on in there..." He flicked her hair. Blonde, straggly wisps trailing down her skinny neck. "Told you, didn't I? I'm the short-arsed kid who put one over the cops." Sassy giggled, riding the clutch, revving hard.

Jackie, thinking: 'Am I the only adult here?' slid on her Belle Cat sunglasses, straightened her white linen skirt and stared out of the window as the Vauxhall shot out of the car park.

Sassy was a nifty getaway driver. Had done a job once with a Newcastle gang and had since affected a Geordie accent. Now she kept pressing Daniel to take her to the flicks to watch Michael Caine in 'Get Carter'.

She raised the subject again while shifting the Vauxhall into the fast lane of the M6..

"He goes North-East for a showdown with the local mob. Guess what he takes with him?"

Daniel said: "A shotgun."

Sassy, miffed: "Know-all."

"Yeah," he laughed. "And he used a Colt 32 in The Ipcress File. Harry Palmer, he was. Yeah, Michael Caine, all tooled up. Mind you, a Colt 32. A peashooter. I want something a lot bigger than that."

"Okay. You mean a Magnum. Like Clint. Dirty Harry. Make my day punk."

"No," Daniel corrected her. "John Dillinger. A Colt 45. Anyway, did you get rid of all the gear?"

She bridled. Swore. "Course I did. Think I'm a novice or summat. Not the PVC though. It fits me just lovely."

Sassy flooring the pedal, grazing 100 mph. Daniel shouting, thumping the dashboard. Jackie, dog tired, snoozing behind the shades.

John Daniel's second heist went badly wrong. "Go!" he shouted, throwing himself into the passenger seat. "And shut her up." Sassy ignored him, concentrating on a sharp left, tyres spinning on the hot, dry tarmac. Daniel had his head in his hands, the kid still bawling her head off. She twisted around and yelled: "Shut up, you little scrag end, or I'll belt you."

The souped-up Mini propelled them out of danger, Sassy slamming it around one road-block, scraping a lamp-post, leaving the sirens behind. Her five years-old daughter, Julie by name, stopped bawling as she eased up.

But Daniel sulked. "Why did you have to bring her?" he moaned.

Sassy was in no mood. "Because your bleedin' mother wouldn't babysit, and as it so happens, she's good for us – an alibi. 'Rob a bank, officer? Us? With a kiddie in the back?' And stop fiddling with that gun, John."

He shoved the pocket-sized Webley under his seat. He looked pale, done-in, reduced by his failure. And she felt it, too. "What went wrong?"

"Dunno. Someone pressed a button, I suppose. Alarms going off. Had to get out. Heard one bastard laughing."

"Maybe they thought it was a toy gun. Just a kid with a toy."

Daniel scowled. "They'll learn." The rest of the journey would have been in morose silence but for a well-worn Jimi Hendrix cassette which Sassy turned up to max and a whining voice from the rear inquiring: "Are we there yet?"

Jackie advised them to lay off for a while. Excluded from active service, she had put on weight, lolling around their flat, eating rubbish, growing resentful.

"I've been thinking about things," she said, wrapped in a dressing gown, feet on the coffee table, one fluffy slipper hanging loose. Sassy turned the radio down – who needed Tony Blackburn anyway? - plonked herself on the sofa, brushed off the crumbs and said: "Get on with it, then."

Jackie bit into a chocolate digestive, provocatively taking her time. "Well, while you two were away, making a mess of everything, a gentleman friend of mine treated me to the cinema. Guess what film?" She crunched. "Dillinger," she announced. "Public Enemy Number One."

"Gentleman?" scoffed Daniel. "Didn't think you knew any."

"No? Well actually, this one has real manners. And he's tall, John. Very tall." And before he erupted: "Does it matter? The point being that I learned something. About robbing banks."

Jackie's message was simple. Planning. Preparation. Dillinger was a real pro.

Daniel chuntered: "Except they shot him full of holes."

Jackie cut in. "Yeah, but our poor bobbies don' t

carry guns. And we'll do it better. You can make a real name for yourself, John, and live the high life. Me, I fancy a place in the sun.". Sassy noticed the glint in his eyes. "Yeah," she said slyly. "And we can take little Julie with us. Family life."

Daniel and Jackie exchanged derisory glances. Sassy was dreaming. The social workers only allowed her occasional access.

"So when do we start?" he asked, casually changing the subject and acknowledging the shift in power.

Between October 1974 and August 1976, amid terrorist bombs, soaring inflation and unemployment and the effing this and effing that of the Sex Pistols, the short-arsed gun-toting robber burst into bank after bank, filling up his mum's Tesco bags. Jackie, posing as a customer, cased the joint each time and Sassy sped them to safety. We in the Press nicknamed him Baby Face after Baby Face Nelson who helped Dillinger to cause mayhem in America's wild and dusty mid-West in the 1930s.

Twice, police thought they had them cornered, only to hear the roar of an engine and the screech of tortured rubber. And when they did slip up, halted for speeding, the patrolman spotted Julie in the back seat, mouth smeared with chocolate. He winked at Sassy. "Take it easy. You've got your kiddie to think about. Right, off you go."

"See," Sassy gloated. "Told you she'd come in useful."

Jackie sneered. "They shouldn't let you have her. A trip to the seaside, is that what you told them? You're no mother." But Sassy was revelling in it. And Daniel was happy, too, with his Colt 45, bought from a canny Glasgow dealer who sniggered: "Only one owner – John Wayne."

Daniel waved it at Sassy. "Better than a pistol."

"You haven't fired it yet."

"When the time comes...."

And, it did. Inevitably. Not the finger pulling the trigger. More like the trigger pulling the finger. Pow! Pow! Pow! Daniel let off three rounds and the cashier's chest exploded, blood splattering the window of his counter.

"You've made it now John," said Jackie, sarcastically, throwing a newspaper at him. "Front page."

She had anticipated disaster. Money put aside, her 'gentleman' waiting at the airport. Dodgy passport, a sunshine villa, but not on the Costa. As the plane approached Rio, she squeezed his hand. "Copacabana. Mmm."

Daniel didn't have an exit strategy. As the net tightened he showed signs of losing control and Sassy told him: "It's over. I'm going to grab Julie and ride into the sunset. Coming?"

He pointed the Colt at her. Then stuck it to his temple.

"No!..."

They found her slumped over his body, sobbing and covered in gore. The story emerged at the inquest when the verdict was 'Suicide while the balance of mind was disturbed'. Soon Sassy was starting a 12 years stretch for armed robbery.

I met her a decade later, hoping to squeeze out enough material for a book. Released on parole, she was slaving in a grimy den run by Ged, a small-time crook who occasionally offered me nuggets for my Crime Buster column in exchange for publicising his Over 60s Outing Fund.

"Do I regret it at all? Yeah. Some bits. But it was exciting for Christ's sake. Like a hot wire running up your veins. I despise people who watch their step, treading through the years like it's all dogshit, worried if they get some on their shoes. That's not life."

We endured a couple of desultory conversations after that, enthusiasm waning on both sides. "Jackie's back," she said one afternoon at her scabby, mould-scented flat.

"And?"

"Well, everyone deserves a second chance. We get on alright. With Ged as well. He lets me use his BMW. It's a blast."

"Brings back memories, eh Sassy? Just tell me one thing – why kill John?"

No answer. Just those eyes, lasering me.

I persisted. "Okay, you wanted out. But you could have walked. Instead you blasted his brains out and made it look like suicide."

Sassy blew a smoke ring, watched it curl lazily to the ceiling. "Baby Face. A good name for him.

Needed mothering. Threatened to shoot me if I tried to leave. Gave me no choice."

She laughed. Knew I could never prove it.

She, Jackie and Ged disappeared soon afterwards. Then, in Newcastle, an armed gang ambushed a Securicor van. A witness said the getaway car accelerated away 'like a rocket'.

But the coveted black PVC coat proved her downfall. She wore it obsessively like wrapping Daniel's ghost around her and, eventually, someone clocked her. She wrote to me from prison just before she hanged herself. "I'm dirt. I know it. But sometimes on a job, I felt like I'd just skinny dipped in a cold pool and washed it all off."

In the early 90s, Julie got in touch via the newspaper. Was I still considering a book about her mum and Baby Face? Could we meet? The city centre wine bar heaved with out-dated Yuppies but she stood out. Slim, Sassy's glittery peepers, Princess Di hair, Gucci shoulder bag. Classy – except for the PVC coat, the cuffs scuffed by steering wheels and gearsticks. She showed me a photo, teenage Sassy smiling, holding a baby. Scrawled on the back 'Love you forever, Mummy'.

"Nice," I said.

"Yeah, she sent it with the details of a safety deposit account. Something about as I'd taken part I deserved my share."

I dropped the book idea and never saw Julie again, although a year later an unsigned postcard arrived, showing a crowded beach and a huge

statue of Christ The Redeemer

TEAM NETTIE

(Essay on the Victorian pioneers of women's football, published by History UK Magazine)

WOMEN'S football was high on the national agenda when England won the European Championship in July 2022. The triumph of the 'Lionesses' was celebrated throughout the country and seen as a watershed moment, specifically for women's sport and, in general, for equal rights.

As Chloe Kelly raced around the Wembley pitch, pulling off her top in a wild celebration after grabbing the winning goal against Germany she might have shouted: "If men can play football so can women," thereby echoing the words of a certain Nettie J Honeyball, long recognised as one of the pioneers of the women's game.

Nettie came to prominence as the founder and secretary of the British Ladies Football Club in 1894. Forming two teams to play each other, their first match at Hornsey in north London on March 23 1895 attracted over 10,000 spectators, mostly men. Riding high on that success, they toured Britain, featuring in over 100 games in the following two years, provoking the wrath of the male Establishment whose criticism ranged from playful jokes about their lack of ability, to full-on broadsides about women needing to 'know their place'.

As one outraged newspaper columnist put it: 'They play in knickers and blouses. They allow the calves of their legs to be seen and wear caps and football boots! What next?'

Well, sir, 127 years later, Chloe Kelly tugged off her shirt, revealing her sports bra, and, instantly, as 90,000 fans inside Wembley and millions of TV viewers shouted and danced in jubilation, it became an iconic image of women's achievements and ambitions. As Nettie J Honeyball once pointed out: "We ladies have too long borne the degradation of prescribed inferiority to the other sex."

The stated objectives of the British Ladies Football Club were:

- to prove that women could play football, but also that they had every right to do so without obstacles being placed in their path;
- to challenge male notions of femininity, particularly in regard to dress – a pet theme of their president, Lady Florence Dixie.

Miss Honeyball also hinted at an element of Suffragism, saying she wanted women in

Parliament, but opinions of the wider political world were generally kept under wraps – the British Ladies Football Club were challenging the male Establishment, but also relying on them for support as they needed grounds to play on and positive publicity in newspapers.

But it is questionable as to whether they fulfilled their mission. It could even be argued that they hampered the progress of women's sport.

The stars of the British Ladies Football Club were, for the most part, poor athletes with little experience of football and scant knowledge of the laws of the game. This may not have mattered if they had worked hard on improving their skills and if not for the fact that they charged admission to their games and paid themselves match fees and 'generous expenses'. Their officials were hard-headed negotiators who haggled over gate money and even took one club to the small claims court over a delayed payment.

To this extent they were thoroughly professional. They made approximately £250 from their debut match.

During 1895 and 1896 they undertook several exhausting tours, covering the length and breadth of Britain, playing two or three matches a week, and staying at temperance hotels. After some games they climbed onto horse-drawn coaches and were hauled through the streets, waving and shouting to onlookers like FA Cup Final winners. But, while curiosity attracted big crowds – 10,000 at the opening fixture and 8,000 in Newcastle and Glasgow – they failed to earn popular, long-term support for the women's game. The perception grew, not only among men, that the public was being taken for a ride.

'The mask has been torn off the British Ladies Football Club' said The Sketch – a newspaper which, originally, had taken a sympathetic view of their efforts. 'It stands revealed as a purely money-making concern'.

Two points backed up The Sketch's accusation in September 1895. Firstly – the standard of the football remained abjectly low provoking laughter and insults and enhancing the view that women could not play. This opinion might have changed if the club had been more serious about improving players' skills, instead they focused on touring and arranging as many fixtures as possible. Secondly – several players had links with the stage. One, Ellie Dunn emerged in later years as the contortionist Miss Lily Flexmore, who wowed audiences in the USA with her leg over the shoulder, foot in the mouth trick. Football club or touring theatre group? The jury was out.

Many questions went unanswered. Some players hid their identities with pseudonyms. It was thought for a long time that Nettie J Honeyball was a Nellie Hudson, but there were two cousins properly named Honeyball, one Annie, one Nellie who could be candidates. As Nellie was later involved in the Suffragism movement, she emerges as the favourite. Ellie Dunn – before concentrating on her 'legmania' act – was R Coupland, goalkeeper Mrs Graham was Helen Matthew. Their best player was 'Daisy Allen', a child thought to be 10-12 years of age and nicknamed Little Tommy by the fans who claimed she was a boy. In fact, she was the daughter of one of the players, Jessie Allen who became the secretary.

That they were brave, adventurous and enterprising is undeniable. They suffered all sorts of abuse in print and from the touchlines, some of it could be described as playful (in the context of the day) but much was grossly insulting, and some so distressing that the police were called in. But they carried on, travelling the length and breadth of Britain by train and steamer, an exhausting campaign of two or three matches a week, sometimes watched by thousands, sometimes a few hundred.

But, in England, if not so much in Ireland and Scotland where they were treated with greater sympathy, a black cloud gathered over the British Ladies Football Club. Critics lashed it as a 'money making exercise', and 'a circus', and the phrase 'fraud on the public' was even used.

While they claimed to practise two or three times a week and to receive coaching from professional male footballers, their standard of play and knowledge of the laws proved sadly lacking. But novelty value assured publicity, large crowds, and gate-money which they split with the host club, usually claiming the larger share. Players received cash and gifts. The BLFC was a professional outfit, providing entertainment of a kind, but not that usually associated with a genuine football club.

Only 'Little Tommy' and Helen Matthews escaped censure. And while it was originally assumed that those with time to play two or three times a week must come from the affluent middle class, Team Nettie included several from more modest environments who presumably needed paying. The question was 'Football club or travelling circus?'

Even so this enthusiastic, adventurous band of sisters might well be remembered as the first 'Lionesses'.

Nettie Honeyball, pioneer of women's football

WINGS OF MAGIC

(Entered for a flash fiction competition, max words 110 - with the prompt 'place')

GOT to get out of here.
Mean streets, grey, threatening.
But how?
"What you doing Mum?"
"Oh, day-dreaming. What's that?"
His plastic collecting box.
"Look" - lifting the lid carefully. "It's rare.
A Clifden. They say it can do magic."
"Wow! A magical moth. Ask it to
fly us to the new estate."
Pain creased his face. He hated change. And
their overgrown garden and creviced brick
walls offered sanctuary to his friends.
Silently, he prayed to the Clifden.
She saw his anguish.
"There again, maybe we can do this place up."
The legendary moth lifted its wings triumphantly.

COLIN EVANS

The legendary Clifden moth

THE SMILING
REFUGEE

*(Entered into the Commonwealth Short Story
prize, max words 5,000 – an immigrant's story)*

STRIPES. That's what hit you on first sight of
Vinu Munshi. Jacket, trousers, shirt, tie, all
sub-divided into thin lengths of dazzling
colour – British racing green, Hindu saffron,
and Ugandan yellow. And a black stripe of a
moustache.

This kaleidoscope of nationalism was a refugee,
one of the 60,000 Asians kicked out of Uganda
by the brutal Idi Amin. One of the 27,000 who
flew into Britain's embrace in the early stage of
the exodus. And the only one to venture further
than the Midlands thanks to a sharp-eyed Home
Office bod who while processing him through
the temporary immigration camp in Surrey
discovered he had written a few articles for a
college newsletter back in Kampala.

And so, via a convoluted circuit of whispers and
the calling in of favours, Vinu Munshi became the

new chief reporter of The Despatch and, as the first black journalist in our region, a propaganda coup.

'Vinu Munshi – an immigrant who has written his own success story,' the government blurb boasted.

Winter 1972/73. Terrorist bombs, strikes, State of Emergency, power cuts. But here was a gleam of Afro/Asian sunshine to lighten the darkness. Who needed storm lamps and candles?

Vinu was 23, well educated and spoke an exquisitely manicured version of the Queen's English. Victoria's rather than Liz 2's but it went down well in our small, deep Blue town. As did his systemic smile and degree first-class in sycophancy.

"Could charm the stripes off a zebra crossing," someone said. Or, perhaps it was just me thinking it.

Then he disappeared. Mrs Webb, his landlady, told me: "Actually, he was very unhappy. Cried sometimes. Said everything was grey and damp. Didn't have a friend. And, well, there was one incident. I'm not going to go into it, but it wasn't very pleasant." Mrs Webb, stooped and grey with hard eyes, rubbing her hands on a pinny. "And, anyway, you weren't that bothered about him then, why now?"

And I never heard anything more of him until recently, 50 years later, when his name cropped up on a FB page. 'Looking to share great memories with old colleagues.'

Great?

I thought what the hell. PM'd him. 'Hello, Vinu. Remember me – Stevie from the Despatch? 1972ish.'

Ping: 'Hi. I'm Shahzeen, Vinu's daughter. It was me who posted – he's not good with keying in and things. Of course, he remembers you. Would love to meet.'

Well, yes, I suppose so. Not that we'd have a lot to talk about. If I recalled rightly, he wasn't into footy, women, or booze. And our lives had gone opposite ways. Apparently, he had quit newspaper work to set up a travel business and was now retired, living in a smart north London suburb while I had retreated, culturally and physically, to a cabin on the wilder shores of Scotland.

Already regretting the contact.

But social media is a whirlpool. Good or bad – it sucks you in. 'OK Shahzeen. I'm due in London for an old codgers' reunion – let's fix something up for then.'

'Thank you Stevie. He'll be so pleased. 'Codgers'?'

*****

Our first few minutes were disconcerting. I recognised him immediately, sat upright at a corner table in a Hampstead cafe. Diminutive, thin and tapered as a snooker cue, immaculately dressed. In stripes, of course, although far more subdued than in his time at the 'Chron', whereas I'd slung on jeans and an old leather jacket after a horrendous night out on the beer. When I said "Vinu", stretching out my hand, he blinked through glasses with thick rims and even thicker lenses and pushed back against his seat as though creating as much distance between us as possible. Did I brush my teeth?

"Stevie," I prompted.

"My God! Stevie. What happened to your hair?"

"We got divorced."

We laughed. Well, he did. But he winced when we finally shook hands. Mine are small but grippy, benefitting from my 100 times a day exerciser to help cope with Carple Tunnel, his hadn't changed. Long, slender stems. Crushable.

"Sorry don't know my own strength."

He was rubbing his wrists. "No. Obviously." He drew down his shirt sleeves, brushed a fleck off his jacket, pushed his phone to one side, giving himself time to draw breath. Soon though, he was back to his smarmy best. He sipped his green tea like a bird, leaning his head into it, then lifting it quickly, chin held high to ensure he didn't spill a drop. I cruised a cup of thick cardamom flavoured coffee, called for another.

"You like Lebanese food then?" he asked, pointing at the menu card.

"Yes. Don't get much chance of it up in the Highlands. But when your Shahzeen asked me to name a rendezvous it was the only place I could think of, at least in this area. Used to stay around here when there were matches at Wembley."

"Ah yes. You were into football, weren't you? And other things."

I wouldn't say it was a sly look, more a 'knowing' one. I frowned. "Like what?"

"Oh. Nothing."

Already it was getting sticky, as I'd feared. For me. But not, perhaps, for him. I had a suspicion it would get worse. For me...

"Excuse me Stevie one moment. When I have to go, I have to go."

"Me too."

The 'Males' was on the other side of the room, the sign scarcely legible even to my laser corrected vision, but he made straight for it, niftily skipping around half a dozen tables. Must have done a recce before I arrived. As agile as ever. No arthritis, then.

For a moment I considered following him, albeit not as adeptly, so we could have a man to man chat over the urinal rather than over the table. But I gave him his privacy and drifted for a minute or two.

Former colleagues yes. But not former mates. Problem was he was a Yes Man with three doffs of the Colonial cap, and, more significantly, brought in as a gimmick, handed a senior role in the newsroom, disregarding his lack of experience but proclaiming the official government line that Brits were happy to accept refugees and to work under them.

Maybe. But not me. I burned. And not from any racist spark. I was all for the melting pot theory. No complaints about immigration either, considering the way we had burgled the Asian and African continents over the centuries. John Bull in a striped jumper, flat cap, mask and a bag emblazoned with 'SWAG' swung over his shoulder striding arrogantly over a pink blotched world atlas.

All very well. But Vinu didn't slot into my idea of a cosmopolitan Britain. Given sanctuary, embraced by our generosity, *my* generosity - and repaying me by grabbing the job which I'd been promised and was mine on merit. Our relationship was taut and solely dependent on his bottomless capacity to soak up the verbals. The cartoon character, constantly splattered against a wall, always coming back for more. Never letting that grin slip. Hang on. He's back from the gents, beaming.

"A good one, was it, Vinu. Full flow. Thirty seconds worth?"

"Ah, Stevie. Always the joker."

He fell silent, inspecting the backs of his hands. "Look, it's not easy to talk here. Why don't you come to our home, meet my family. A bit more comfy."

"How. Have you got lots of toilets?"

He waited, Patiently, politely.

"Ok, but it will have to be tonight. I'm off home tomorrow. Ten hours drive north. No, make it 12. Forgot about the M6 on a Friday."

We agreed an 8pm slot. "Just a coffee. No grub, thanks. My guts need some R and R."

Vinu smiled. "Of course."

We paused outside the door, almost fell into a

man hug only for Vinu to withdraw at the last moment, possibly to dodge my breath or avoid some over zealous squeezing. His frail frame quick stepped towards the Northern Line tube. I meandered back to my B and B to prepare myself for the onslaught.

Munshi Mansion was a five bedroomed 1930s detached in Hendon, the drive covered with tarmac and a palette of vanity vehicles, two SUVs, chilli red and indigo, acting as bouncers for a British racing green Mini Cooper. The false door knocker was a chrome-plated replica of Idi Amin. I rang the bell, giving the security camera a brief wave.

"Oh, come in, Stevie. Welcome." An attractive if heavily made-up 40 something in a sea green and Kola gold sari. Hoops rather than stripes but definitely a la famille.

"Oh, you don't need to," Shahzeen said as I kicked my trainers off.

"Well, I do. It's custom. Anyway, I do the same at my place."

A long hallway lined with orthodoxy. Black framed family photos. Then an 8m x 6m warehouse faking it as a living room virtue of two giant-sized sofas, a cinema screen and an automatic 'Wow!' from every guest.

Bedazzled, sort of, I didn't even spot Vinu until a figure rose from the cushions.

"Stevie." brushing fingertips. He'd learned.

"Some place you have here, Vinu."

"Yes, a family home. We all have a stake in it."

"Puts mine in the shade somewhat."

"Well, what is it that we British say. Each to their own."

It had started.

Shahzeen butted in. Thank you Shahzeen. "Look, we eat at 9. OK? So think on, an hour to yourselves and then the thali."

I glared at Vinu. No grub? A real thali, and this would be 100 per cent proof, could last for hours with limitless top-ups of rice, bread, curries, pickles, all washed down with buckets of buttermilk. Vinu shrugged.

"Our hospitality," he murmured.

"In the meantime," Shahzeen continued pleasantly, "Drinks. There's whisky or a beer perhaps. Or I make a top drawer lassi. Maybe best – Papa said you'd had a rough night."

"Yes, but I think I'll go traditional British. So a beer please."

She had a way of clutching her sari with her right hand. I saw it clench, the silk tightening. "Water for you Papa?" But it wasn't really a question. He nodded but she'd already turned away.

We sat opposite, drinks on the huge carved coffee table which kept us too far apart for bad breath to be an issue. "Such a good girl. Looks after us all. Family is everything, don't you think?"

"Certainly. Apart from those who kill each other."

"A bit cynical, heh?"

I let it ride. "You've obviously done well, Vinu."

"Thank you. You know, when Amin expelled us, we arrived here with nothing. He gave us 90 days to get out, one suitcase each and some cash, about £50. Can you imagine that?" He sniffed. "After all we'd done for Uganda."

"Terrible," and, for once, I meant it. I hadn't fully understood back in the Seventies – who did? - but I had a few facts up my sleeve after a quick internet search. How Britain had induced Indian businessmen to migrate to Uganda, how they had backed Amin to seize power and the panic when they realised he wasn't the right type at all. In brief – another almighty strategic cock-up.

"Madman wasn't he? Soldier, president, mass murderer, cannibal – wasn't that the progression? Kept severed heads in his fridge. So how come he's got pride of place on your front door"

"Ha! My idea. Shahzeen's design. A reminder that when one door slams in your face another one opens. We wcre homeless only for a short while." Vinu paused.

"So Stevie. All those who come to our door are welcomed. I hope you appreciate that."

He swallowed water. Set his glass down, a little too hard.

For the last couple of weeks I'd geared myself up for Retribution Day. Poor Vinu had waited over half a century. So no rush. More of the back story...

"Kampala 1972," Vinu datelining it like a front page lead. "Amin had a dream. A nightmare more like. Said that Allah wanted Uganda to be returned to the indigenous people. Can you imagine God ordering ethnic cleansing!?

"Our family. Six of us with Nana. Had a lovely villa. Verandah, red tiles, garden with jasmine. Dad had worked hard. Like all his business colleagues. The economy was booming but Amin said we had sabotaged it. Crazy. Anyway, at first, we thought it was some weird joke. Everyone knew that if we left the country would crash. But then.."

I waited. I'd never really liked Vinu. Superficial. A deflector, casually warding off the blows with a flick of his wrists, or a twist of the lips. But this was something else. How old was he? Mid seventies definitely. Should you weep at that age? I wasn't sure. All I know is that he took off his specs, grabbed a tissue from the box on the table, and dabbed the corners of his eyes.

"Yes, well," replacing the glasses. "Where was I? Ah, of course. I'm not boring you?"

He wasn't. And, even if I'd said yes, he would have carried on. It was there, had to come out.

"A joke, it wasn't. They came late one night. Soldiers. Smashed their way in. Told us to pack. Nana tried to collect some photographs, precious, but they laughed, piled them up, burnt them in front of her. Dad protested and got a kick in the stomach for his trouble. They dragged my sister into the street and abused her. She was 14."

My face must have registered. "No, not that. But they beat her, said dreadful things. Dreadful. One of them used his rifle to pull her dress up and she stopped crying because she was so scared. We couldn't do anything. They had guns. The trucks came, perhaps saved her, and took us to the airport. She was never the same."

My stomach gurgled loudly, the acids still battling with the previous night's excesses. Note to self. No more reunions based on all day alcohol and midnight Mexicana tacos with extra hot sauce.

I saw Vinu wincing as though in sympathy. "Sorry. Didn't mean to interrupt so rudely. You were saying - the day they shunted you. Did they tell you where you were headed?"

He feigned surprise, mouth open, thick eyebrows rising, arms spread. "What? They didn't need to. We were British citizens. Don't you know your glorious Colonial history? My parents were Indian, proud members of the Empire." Sarky. Not smiling now. In fact he had barely smiled all evening.

"Britain had to take us. They'd put us in Uganda in the first place. Had given us the blue passport, the key to the world. We arrived here on a plane, not a small boat. Dad joked about it. 'Hey, son, don't despair. We're going home!' Ha!. Then we landed at Stansted and my knees were knocking, it was that cold. And that flat, colourless landscape. I thought 'some home.'

Vinu leaned back, one arm spread over the back of the sofa, spindly legs crossed. I waited.

"Strange, isn't it," he said. "We were evicted, came here. Now all you hear about is Britain's immigration problems while Uganda takes in more immigrants than any other country in the world. Sometimes I wonder if we'll get sent back."

Noise in the kitchen, voices, the banging and scraping of pans. My last thali, a real one not the scam served up as a veggie alternative in your local carvery, was in India's industrial city of Ahmedebad where at 'The Gujurat Canteen' I was urged to 'Eat, eat', the mounds of food continually replenished by staff ladling it from huge pots carried on a metal yoke across their shoulders. No way would I survive the one being created by Shahzeen. My insides lurched. Should have gone for the lassi instead of the beer. Vinu appeared not to notice my discomfort. Or simply ignored it.

I wanted out. If he had something to say and he had, of course he had, why not spit it out.

"Look old pal, I need to be…"

Too late. He was back on track.

"It wasn't easy. The job offer came out of the blue. I didn't really want to go north. London seemed fine. But the family pushed. So there I was, the only black man in town. Your town. Putting on a face to get through the day. But you never really thought about it like that. Otherwise you wouldn't have done what you did."

Uh-uh. Wait for it.

Vinu had taken off his glasses again, holding them loosely in his left hand, his right playing with the tassels of a vivid orange cushion, eyes slipping out of focus. Suddenly he lunged forward, grabbed the glass, smashed it on the table edge. Water splashed, blood spurted.

"Jesus!"

"This is what you did." He placed the remains of the tumbler, holding it by the base, against his wrist.

"See those marks." He had levered up his shirt cuff. I recalled him pulling it down in the cafe as though to hide something. Scars which looked pale against his skin, rising three inches from just above the thumb joint.

"I couldn't stand it any more. Mrs Webb, the landlady? A lovely lady. She saved me. Bandaged me up, got me to the Cottage Hospital. I was exceedingly grateful."

He held his damaged hand, blood seeping through his fingers and laughed.

"Those anonymous letters you wrote. Stirring up trouble. Saying I was - what was it? Oh yes: 'One of the foreign freeloaders taking our jobs'. It was you, wasn't it? And people responded didn't they? Began ignoring me, giving me funny looks.

"But everything leads to where you are. And I'm here. With my family. And this – it's worth over £2million." His hands swept the room. Blood dripped onto the blue velvet sofa. "And what have you got Stevie? On your own, now, are you? Getting older isn't easy on your own. The days creeping in."

 If nothing else I've learned to act cool under fire. So once the initial shock had dissipated – thanks as much to his high-pitched, squeaky laugh as anything – I felt in control. Although the glass shards glittered a warning.

"Shame there isn't a Cottage Hospital near here, Vinu. I could take you to the Middlesex if you like, if you promise not to get blood all over my car."

A joke. He just didn't share my humour.

"Shahzeen will take me. See yourself out – I expect you're not in the mood for eating."

"Hardly the most enticing appetiser, I must admit. So no. I'll be on my way." He was calling for his daughter.

"Incidentally, I didn't write the letters. I just put the idea into someone's head. Regretted it almost straight away but too late – he had already dipped his pen into the poison. For him it was just a bit of a laugh. But that's how it can start, I suppose."

He grunted, shouted: "Shahzeen!"

I was on my feet, ready to go but plonked myself down again. He'd had his say. I wanted mine. Blood or no blood. And, in truth, there wasn't much of it anyway. I wondered about his suicide bid at Mrs Webb's. Touch of attention seeking? Yeah. "So, as we're not eating, here's something to chew on. Fact is I'd been promised that job. I wanted it, needed it, deserved it.

"There was I celebrating with the missus. Forked out for a bottle of Mateus Rose and you popped up. Out of nowhere. A grinning cat from some strange exotic land for us all to pet. Front page in the Despatch. 'Refugee Makes His Own Headline.' Nice pic. Big smile. But there was no merit in it. You were clueless. It was all political."

"Don't know what you mean."

"Don't you? Really? Okay. Just a pawn you were my friend. I reckon it went like this. Some Smart Alec in the Home Office discovers you've done a few months as a trainee on the Kampala Heritage Centre monthly newsletter or whatever, and cooks up a publicity stunt. The first black journalist in the North. A real boost to Britain's democratic, inclusive image. Can't ever accuse us of racism. A word to the wise here, a word there, and it's all sorted. And..."

Vinu jumped up, banging his knee on the coffee table, bent to clutch it with his good hand, releasing his hold on the injured one, and moaned in despair as more blood dripped, this time onto the deep pile, cream carpet.

I watched with a measure of satisfaction.

"And, you weren't that naive. You knew I'd been stitched up. And I had to grin and bear it, didn't I? Cover up for you every time you fell down on the job. Couldn't have people thinking the black superstar was a right pillock."

"Oh God," he whispered. "Ambulance."

"Bollox. I'm not Mrs Webb. It's just a wee cut, nothing serious."

Shahzeen rushed in, breathless. "I heard you shouting but I was in the bathroom and.. Oh! What's happened? Papa?"

"A and E."

She stared wide-eyed at him, then at me, grabbed

his arm, checked the wound. "I'll get a plaster. I don't believe this. It's all over the place. The sofa. Oh no, not the carpet."

*****

Three months later Vinu and I stood on the edge of my fly fishing secret. A remote lochan with a tough 40 minutes walk-in, leaving Shahzeen in the Land Rover, content with a book and views over rolling hills and Western seas. He'd surprised me with his stamina, climbing strongly to 1000 feet and then striding out through rough bell heather, bog and tussocks of cotton grass, pausing only for me to rest nagging joints.

"Kampala is all hills," he said.

"Yeah, but it was a long time ago. You don't still miss it, surely?"

"Twinges. Politics aside. But you know this isn't bad. Hell, is that an eagle!?"

It was, soaring above the ridge, its huge wings shadowing the sun sparkled water.

"I understand why you live here," he said.

"I'm glad you came. We don't see many black millionaires in these parts. Also Vinu."

"What?"

"We've talked. Still things to resolve, no doubt some arguments, but at least we're getting closer."

He turned to me, put his hand on my shoulder. "Yes, Chinese philosophy – to find the middle ground, you must go back and forth, back and forth."

"Aye."

We watched the eagle circling overhead, rising high on the thermals.

PARIAH DOG

(Entered for a historical fiction prize, max words 3,500 – a dark tale of the 1857 Indian Mutiny)

IF you take the following to be a confession, please reconsider, for what is the purpose of confession but to repent and beg forgiveness. I offer not contrition, nor seek understanding and so accept that Yama will sling his noose around my neck, bind me to his buffalo and drag me into the fiery pit of Naraka. And will they all be watching? Sometimes, at night, as the never-ending cremation smoke mingles with the cold mist of Mother Ganga, I see them, floating over the water, eyes wide-open. Edmund Avery, Benares, 1878.

*****

July 1857, Ashokabad, Central India:
Cornelius Beauchamp was never the most elegant of men. Some mocked him. He needed a woman. To smooth the creases out of his clothes, to trim the remnants of his rapidly disappearing hair, to flick the crumbs from his moustache, but Beauchamp had lived a solitary life and, now, crumpled, bloody, his pale face contorted, he was more dishevelled and more alone than ever. Blood

had surged from his throat onto his shirt, masking the everyday stains which marked him as a struggling bachelor.

Shakespeare bent forward to touch him, then stood upright peering at his own blood-smudged fingertip, and pronounced: "Almost dry. Dead for a few hours, I think." He ordered the chuprassi to fetch the Colonel. "At the double! Challo! Juldi!", the commands followed by a clip across his head. The terrified boy sped away, shouting: "Hatya, hatya!"

"Shut the door." Shakespeare was authoritative and nimble-minded. Alternatively, bossy and cunning. But, while the Telegraph Office of the British Residency in Ashokabad was my domain, he was the Adjutant, the Agent's right-hand man, and so I obeyed, plunging us into a fetid gloom. Flies covered Beauchamp's chest. Outside, where vultures wheeled, he would have been cleaned up for the first time in his life, his bones gleaming bright in the sun.

Shakespeare swept the bluebottle swarm away, but within seconds they were feasting again and he turned away. "Disgusting. This is the work of the Devil, and if the Devil is some disaffected, malcontent native, I'll have him blown to Kingdom Come." I let him prattle on. It was the obvious reaction, blame it on the 'heathens', but I kept quiet. Shakespeare hadn't long been in India, hopefully he would change, although I had my doubts.

"Talking of which," - Shakespeare, interrupted by

the 'boom' of a cannon in the distance, looked at me quizzically. "What in Inferno's name was that?" I pulled the door open. Another 'boom', the sound of horses, someone shouting in Hindi: 'Death to the Feringhees', and a woman screaming.

"Mutiny!" I shouted, grabbing Shakespeare by the shoulder. "This is the first place they'll attack. They hate the telegraph. We've got to get out of here."

"What about Beauchamp?!"

"Leave him. He's dead. We've got to stay alive. And I've got to find Mary."

As I rushed towards our bungalow 50 yards away, I was overtaken by three native cavalry. A flash of a sabre, a searing pain across my back, and I tumbled into the dust while they rode on. I heard: "Edmund!" and looked up. Mary was running, but towards me and into the path of the horsemen instead of to safety. She went down and the last thing I saw before losing consciousness was her arm raised up, pleading, as they hacked away at her.

But no. I have tried in so many ways to put it behind me, to forget, but that wasn't the last thing. The vision which has haunted me ever since was of Mary's severed head, swinging slightly, her killer gripping her long fair hair as he cantered away, laughing. And her eyes staring at me, full of reproach. When I fully regained my senses, I was on the back of a bullock cart, rumbling over a rutted track with Shakespeare offering me a flask.

"Drink this, old boy. Thought you had bought it,

but I got to you in the nick of time." The sun was going down behind a veil of dust.

"Where's my wife?" My voice creaked along with the cartwheels.

"Don't worry about that," said Shakespeare. "We made it. That's the important thing."

*****

And so how does one live when his wife's skull lies forlorn in some poppy field, those once remorseful eyes now empty, black sockets, the teeth bared as though hissing contempt, and strands of fair hair trailing in the cloying black soil of Malwa? I never loved Mary. But she was mine. Like the carved marble chess set, and my atlas, and my soft leather riding gloves. All looted from me, leaving such a bare, arid existence.

*****

May 1858, Ashokabad:

"The Illustrated London News," stated Sir George Malcolm, flourishing the journal at me. The new man in charge of Ashokabad - the 'Agent' - looked at ease at his desk in the Residency, leaning back in his chair, one booted leg stretched out. His predecessor, Colonel Stelfox, had always sat upright, stiff-backed, as an example of British discipline.

"Make yourself comfortable, Avery," said Malcolm. "It has published the official list of the dead." He paused, anticipating a response and, when I failed him, he went ahead anyway. Why, I'm not sure. We knew the list of victims by heart. In the 'Illustrated' it appeared in alphabetical order. "Avery, Mary. Killed by mutineers. Killed!'" He was working himself into a rage as though castigating my own lack of emotion. Stoic, people called me. Malcolm roared on: "Killed!? More like butchered. Avery, your poor wife." His eyes were moist, his nostrils twitched. But he got no change from me.

"Let me continue. Beauchamp, Cornelius. Killed by mutineers."

Not really, I thought.

Over 50 Europeans died in the massacre, cut down like Mary, or shot, or blown to pieces by grapeshot from a rebel cannon, and Malcolm was chewing over the details of each victim like a hook-nosed scavenger when I begged his leave. "I have a lot of work to catch up on, sir," I said. He waved me out.

The Residency enclave was filled with the sound of hammers and saws as construction workers restored burned-out buildings, the Treasury, the Cutcherry, the Chapel and the Opium Store, but it was nothing compared to the throbbing drumbeat in my head which measured my every step. While the sabre cut across my back had healed into an ugly weal, I couldn't sleep, had lost weight and my hair, once reddish-brown, was streaked with grey. Malcolm was sympathetic but Shakespeare did not skirt the issue. "You need a break. Get up into the hills. Fresh air, wonderful panoramas."

I shook my head: "There's a job to be done."

Shakespeare balanced his hat on the tip of his cane and whirled it overhead like a spinning top. "You're an eager beaver, aren't you?" he said. "But if you're looking for promotion, think again. You're not the right type, old sport." A reference to my modest upbringing, no doubt. But I wasn't concerned about my career. I suspected we had been betrayed, that a traitor had slashed Beauchamp's throat, that Mary and the others had died as a result. I intended to seek him out, like a pariah dog rummaging for old bones.

Many Britons quit India after the horror of the 1857 uprising but, after our escape, having washed up in Bombay, Shakespeare and I were back in Ashokabad to help the official investigation into the massacre. Shakespeare was of little use. While I conducted interviews and wrote reports, he led wildlife hunts and punitive expeditions into the scorched countryside, burning villages and hanging natives. I didn't remonstrate. The people of the Central India plains were suffering Britain's version of the 'wrath of God' for the mutiny. Thousands of withered bodies hung from the trees. At a distance they looked like flocks of roosting crows. "Sometimes," said Shakespeare wistfully, "if you nab enough of them you can create patterns, like a figure of eight."

Preparing a concise, accurate report of the events at Ashokabad was impossible. Memories were skewed by prejudice or blanked by fear. However I held one significant piece of evidence, a telegram from the Governor of Bombay marked 'Secret', saying that 'received intelligence' warned of treachery in our camp and an imminent uprising. It was dated July 1, 1857 and timed at 4am, five hours before the massacre and when Beauchamp was the only employee in the office. He always volunteered for night duty, enjoying the quiet.

Someone had executed him to prevent the telegram being delivered to Colonel Stelfox. Why they hadn't taken it with them, I don't know, perhaps they were disturbed, or they simply didn't think it mattered, that by the time it was discovered it would be too late. And they were right. I'd prised it from Beauchamp's cold grip just as Shakespeare burst through the door, answering my shouts for help, and shoved it into an inside pocket where it still lay, curled at the edges and tinged with treacherous yellow. Unaware of its existence, Malcolm ordered me to wrap up the investigation at the double, while Shakespeare opined there was nothing new to discover, adding: "Don't overlook the obvious."

Which was?

The natives. Obviously. 'Savages' who didn't appreciate what the Empire had done for them. Not for the first time he drank copious amounts of brandy and soda, constantly admonishing me for my restraint. "They chopped off your wife's head for God's sake!" Others agreed with him. I steered a lonely trail after that.

When it came to interrogating a bunch of sepoy mutineers held in a makeshift but heavily guarded cell adjacent to the Cutchery, he left me to it, deferring to my superior command of native languages. "Go to it, old boy," he jeered as he rode off on another hunting sortie. "Rack 'em."

Setting up a desk outside the Cutcherry, I had the prisoners brought out, one by one. All displayed surprising defiance, standing to attention, calling out their regiment, name and rank, then refusing to speak despite my threats and finger-wagging. I was tired and frustrated. "We will hang you like the washing on a line," I ranted at the last man, senior to the rest, a havildar named Salim. He smiled and, with heavy sarcasm, stated: "We are at your service, Sahib." But, where the others had gazed over my head, as though I didn't exist, this officer looked me straight in the eye.

"There is something more?", I asked quietly.

He glanced towards the cell where his comrades were huddled, no doubt with ears pricked. He held my gaze again, then screeched: "Death to all Feringhees."

That night, pretending to be the worse for drink and armed with a cane, I told the sergeant on guard to haul Salim out of the cell to be flogged. "I think he was the tyrant who killed my dear Mary," I explained. Austin was a hard-bitten veteran who had taken part in the brutal ransacking of the city of Jhansi. "I'll give you a hand, Mr Avery," he said, grunting with anticipation. We pulled Salim around the back of the Cutcherry. I slapped him across the head while Austin booted him viciously in the ribs, singing lines from 'The Sweet Banks of

Dundee' between each kick.

"Thank you, sergeant," I said, holding him by the arm. "I don't think he's in any shape to resist now. Leave it to me, will you? It's personal." Austin gave Salim another dig with his boot, spat on him and walked away, whistling. The havildar was hurt, all the wind taken out of him. I whispered: "I think you have something to tell me."

Still gasping from Austin's onslaught, he whimpered: "I have a wife. And five children. You will plead for me?"

"Of course. Now talk."

What Salim revealed left us both breathless. I pushed him back to the cell, thanked Austin for his co-operation, returned to the bungalow, and sank exhausted into my wicker chair. Pitch black night, dogs howling, mosquitoes whirring. Despite the humidity I shivered, and wondered whether I was in the early grip of fever. My sleep was deeply troubled by a familiar dream. Mary's head glided gracefully through the night like a Chinese lantern, her face bright, her gaze fixed on me. When she drifted away, there was no respite, for the sky was then filled with countless more heads, dark, mouths wide open in silent horror. The ghosts of Sarawak where, under the flag of righteous Imperialism, the 'White Rajah', James Brooke had painted the hills and dyed the estuaries a vivid red with the blood of thousands of Dayak natives. Backed by the British government he made war on naked tribesmen, armed with spears and bows. And I helped him. Officially I was there as a clerk, but when Brooke ordered you to exchange pen and paper for sword and rifle you obeyed.

And, the truth was (for there is no point now in self-deceit) I revelled in it. The thrill of adventure. During this period, a sepoy taught me how to kill in the style of the Thuggees, the Indian robbers who preyed on travellers, strangling them with neckerchiefs, knotted and weighted with a coin. A useful technique I found in taking village guards by surprise.

The feel of it. More rewarding than a bullet or a blade. The cloth whirling around his throat, the tightening and twist. Strength was needed, but timing was the key. I became an expert. They jokingly called me 'Thuggee Sahib'.

As usual, I woke up violently, sweat streaming off me. Over breakfast I told Malcolm and Shakespeare that the six prisoners had readily confessed to their crimes. We all knew differently, of course, but Malcolm nodded assent while spooning marmalade onto his toast. As the sun began its slide in the west, the sepoys were hanged on a hastily constructed gallows and a field gun was hauled onto the parade ground. A boy drummer tapped out the signal, and Salim was escorted across the compound, placed at the cannon's mouth and tied. He sneered at me, refused a blindfold, appealed to Allah, and was blown away, one of his hands falling from the sky like a shot pigeon, spraying blood on my shoulder.

"Good show," said Shakespeare, shaking my hand.

"Now they understand British justice."

I smiled.

"Yes, Shakespeare. Hard but fair, and the Lord is on our side."

For once, he seemed uncertain of what to say, then turned and strode towards the Residency.

To count on Salim's word alone was cavalier. But it worked out. I just had to bide my time and the chance came when Malcolm was called to Calcutta for a conference. In his absence and with Shakespeare drinking heavily, security grew lax. One night, having excused myself from dinner in the Residency, I inserted a Madras silver rupee into a neckerchief, slipped it into my waistband, and waited. Near midnight I edged out of the bungalow, and, via a circuitous route through abandoned gardens, across ditches, and over crumbling walls, I reached my destination. Embers of cooking fires cast shadows over this part of the compound but heavy cloud hid the moon. If anyone saw me enter, they stayed mute and, inside, darkness enfolded me. An hour or so later I heard a voice calling "Goodnight" and someone stumbled on the veranda, laughing to himself. Seconds later he came through the door, fiddled with a lamp, and sat on a chair. As he bent to take off his boots, I lunged from behind, the neckerchief twirling.

"And that is British justice for you, Shakespeare," I

said. His eyes bulged.

'Turncoat,' Salim had murmured, stupidly believing it would earn him a reprieve. "Shakespeare, Sahib, turncoat.'

Deflecting suspicion was easy as Malcolm put me in charge of the investigation. Several innocents from the bazaar were summarily hanged and shops fired to persuade people to name the killer. Of course, none did.

Shakespeare cut Beauchamp's throat and betrayed his fellow countrymen, of that I was sure. Essentially, he murdered Mary. But his plan went awry. The rebels promised him wholesale butchery, the whole camp and its occupants destroyed in a matter of minutes, but, after the initial onslaught, they veered into a looting and burning rampage enabling a handful or Europeans to get clear. Suddenly vulnerable, he picked me off the floor, dragged me through the smoke to the Residency and joined the escape party, acclaimed as a hero.

But why the betrayal? His motivation eluded me until the chaplain remarked after his funeral: "Poor Shakespeare. But his heart was never in India - he merely wanted to make his fortune out here and pay off the family debts." Obviously, he had sold his loyalty. To whom exactly and for how much wasn't really important. His granite headstone said: 'Augustus Dionysus Shakespeare, Adjutant, Ashokabad, born 1827, died on duty May 28 1858'. Malcolm asked me to draft a letter of condolence to his family who were struggling to maintain large estates in Oxfordshire. "You knew him better than me. He saved your life, didn't he?"

*****

December 1882, Benares:
When I cough now, there is blood in the spittle.

*****

I left Ashokabad for good after things had calmed down, joined the new Indian Civil Service, and then quickly left that. Too British, by far, old sport. After all, while my father was English, my mother was a native woman, and I was born and bred in India. Its dust coats my veins. Eventually, I heeded Shakespeare's advice to take to the hills and, over the years, as I climbed higher, I gradually disabused myself of British garb, manners, and, finally, faith. As they say, I 'went native'. But perhaps Shakespeare has had the last laugh. Maybe he sent me to my death, for it was in the thin, damp mountain air that I became so ill, and now I have returned to the insufferably hot plains to die on the banks of Mother Ganga. Here on the holy ghats of Benares, I bathe daily, dipping my head three times, and pray to Lord Shiva (or whatever god takes my fancy). And, while the nightmares are ever there, Mary's reproach has softened. I have come to a passiveness, an acceptance. Years after my departure from Ashokabad, a dog, scratching for buried bones just outside the Residency grounds, unearthed a skull with a wisp of fair hair attached. They buried it (or should that be 'her'?)

in the cemetery. Surely, angels welcomed Mary, a gentle soul, at the Pearly Gates. I must take my chances with Yama and his buffalo and I have paid good money to ensure that the timber for my pyre is properly dry and aged, so that it burns fiercely.

◆ ◆ ◆

The Telegraph Office at Indore, Central India where Cornelius Beauchamp was found murdered in 1857.

THE FEATHERS

(For a flash fiction prize, max words 50
- with the prompt 'feathers')

Could murder a pint
Me too
Let's try The Feathers
Yeah – happy memories
Such as?
It's where I shot my husband
Wow!
Yeah. I'm out on parole
Wasn't on the date app profile
No. Want to see the gun?
Got it with you?
Yeah. He survived, but not this time.

◆ ◆ ◆

The 'gun' possibly a .32 Colt double action revolver, only 5-6 inches long and easily concealed in a pocket or handbag, designed for travellers and ladies out on a date...

DEATH ON THE GRAPEVINE

*(An entry for a crime fiction competition,
max words 4,000 – think 1960s)*

O F the dozen wreaths which lay sopping wet and forlorn against the marble headstone, the one which caught my attention was a cheaper type from the florist opposite the cemetery, a ring of fading red roses weaved into a base of heather and twisted hazel. Pinned onto it, an In Memoriam card decorated by an out of focus photo of a footballer and the message 'On the wing to Heaven – J C's Forever Fan Club'.

Only a handful had turned up, sporting their red and white scarves which stood out amid the funereal black. Whether any of them cried was difficult to tell - the dark rain had hammered down, masking all emotion while the graveside ceremonies were hastily disposed of, his widow encouraging everyone to get it over with 'before we all drown'.

I had already interviewed Myra Challinor. She appeared street-wise, hard-bitten, and not particularly fond of the man she had just buried, an impression enhanced by one of his supporters who approached me, saying: "Jimmy could have been a big star." She hesitated, checking out Myra who was hurrying towards an undertaker's car. "If he'd had the right people around him." She pulled her scarf tighter and walked away.

The phone box outside the cemetery's main gate stank of urine and was plastered with prostitutes' calling cards. Thai, Swedish, or straight down the line British – what better than a relaxing massage after saying farewell to a loved one? Thankfully, the Evening Despatch's copy-taker was red-hot on the keys. Ten paragraphs filed in no time, a quick word with Fred on the news desk, and I was out, sucking in fresh air, gratefully lifting my face to the rain. At a nearby newsagent's, a Despatch billboard shouted 'World Cup glory for our boys' - England had reached the final. Another revealed: 'Murdered footballer tortured'.

The story was that two of the world's hopeless, searching for a safe place to drown some amphetamines with a bottle of cheap vodka, had discovered Jimmy Challinor's body under a rotting barge hulk by a disused canal which trickled past abandoned wharves and warehouses. Fred had joked: "They see a toecap, pull it and out pops a corpse." Chuckles all around. Journalism was a crude, cynical environment. I cherished it.

Summer 1966. Britain's Swinging Sixties. Oh, yeah. A lot of rose-tinted dross has been written about that era. The Cultural Revolution was roaring along, sweeping tradition aside like torn-up betting slips, but it wasn't all happy-clappy. The economy was crumbling and organised crime rising with Jimmy one of its victims, ripped by razors and, burnt by cigarette ends. Why?

Years back, Jimmy was a nippy player, a winger and a crowd favourite at a second-tier club but, when his career was prematurely wrecked by a heart condition, he plummeted into debt and became enmeshed in the barbed wire periphery of the sporting world, dingy back-street boxing gyms, murky nights at the dog track. No doubt, his killers lurked in this shadowland but the police investigation had stalled.

Driving from the cemetery I thought of Myra. Would she agree to another interview? The first, conducted on the doorstep of their neat suburban semi, was short and sour. "I'd warned him that he was mixing with the wrong people," she muttered, arms folded, staring me down. Myra was mid 30s, slim, dark-haired, make-up adeptly applied. Hardly the grieving type. And, while I couldn't put my finger on it, there was something else. Like she was converting the step into a stage. Yes, worth another visit.

I parked the rusting 12 years-old Ford Popular at the 'Acropolis' and used a side door to reach my upstairs bedsit. From below came the clatter of crockery and the hazy murmur of customers tucking into the midweek special of steak pie, chips, peas and gravy (3s 6d), served up against an incongruous backdrop of artificial vines, bunches of grapes hanging from the walls and ceiling and cheap plastic framed pictures of ancient Greek ruins. Gloria would be serenading the chip fryer with a Nana Mouskouri ballad, Joe wobbling his belly fat to wring a smile from the doughty library lady, who lunched there each Wednesday to escape the numbing silence she worked in.

Here was an oasis in a creeping desert of demolition sites and wasteland. The city and its history were being reconstructed amid clouds of dust and grit and broken lives as the bulldozers rumbled forward. Whole streets torn down, thousands of bemused refugees force-marched from the comfort zones of their scruffy terraces towards grey anonymous blocks of high-rise flats, or sprawling 'overspill' estates in alien countryside. A bright new future, they were told. But, in homage to its namesake, the Acropolis survived. "We used to call it The Golden Fry, then I took Gloria on a holiday to Athens," Joe explained. "Never been the same since." After a few ouzos, she would dance to an LP of bouzouki music, swirling around their living room floor only to collapse onto their purple-fringed sofa, misquoting Plato as if to prove she was once an Education Officer.

Two days after the funeral, with the news desk

screaming at me to get my finger out and produce a decent piece, I returned to Myra's. This time she invited me in. A leather suite, a 24 inches Pye TV and a smart, mahogany radiogram filled the lounge. She registered my surprise. "Jimmy bought it all. Last thing he did for us. Let's go into the kitchen."

We perched on high stools. When I overbalanced while accepting a cup of coffee, she laughed harshly, "Men – useless," and threw me a dishcloth to mop up the drips. A packet of menthol-tipped cigarettes lay on the table. 'Cool as a mountain stream', so their advert said. Suited Myra to a T.

"Where did Jimmy get the money from?" I asked. "The furniture, I mean."

"No idea. Don't care." She stared out of the window. An overgrown back garden, a rickety greenhouse in the corner. She turned towards me. "We went back a long way, me and Jimmy. But it was never good. Always talking big. Always on the make. And he could get nasty."

You and him both, I thought. "But you stuck together," I offered, more to cut through the tension than in the hope of eliciting a considered response.

"Yeah, well, you get used to things, don't you?" She was again gazing through the window but at a murky past rather than at the garden, her face hardening, warding off the demons. "It's like this - when you're a kid you get belted every day so you think it's normal, when you're married he comes home pissed, demanding his tea, slapping you about because it's gone cold, and it's normal, happens to everyone, doesn't it? That's what you tell yourself, but you know really it's not right, because you try to hide the bruises so no-one asks questions, and when they do, you say you tripped up or had a fight with a door, and they say 'oh, ok' because, actually, it is normal."

She lit a cig, and offered me one which I refused. "Oh, you don't. Don't suppose you have any vices." That rankled. I was no naive goody-goody but I let it go. She smoked, I sipped the thin, lukewarm coffee, promising myself a decent cup later at the Acropolis. Gloria's was strong, and sweet, sometimes flavoured with cardamom. Myra broke the silence. "Jimmy was a loser. That's the fact of it. Write what you like." A hiss of bile. "I don't give a damn. Now get out." So, I did.

It made the front page. "Wow, let's celebrate," said Joe, when I triumphantly shoved the paper under his nose. "Okay - but not ouzo, for Christ's sake. And not bloody Nana Mouskouri."

Their flat was on the ground floor behind the cafe. I took control of the Dansette record player, ignored Gloria's protests, and turned The Who up loud. Soon we were all jigging away, bellowing out 'My Generation', Gloria, hands in the air, fag in one, her specs fogged up, giving extra bite to Roger Daltrey's 'Why don't you all f...f... fade away?'.

*****

One of the low dives frequented by Jimmy

Challinor was a drinking den close to the cathedral but a million miles from any kind of salvation. Jez Parrott, the owner, had a sense of humour – he called it The Peacock because it lacked any colour or pride. He rejected my suggestion of The Cage. Jez and I had history. For example, he craved publicity for the club's 'Over 60s Outing Fund', which facilitated a weekend of seaside debauchery for him and two mates – 'Well, they're both over 60' – and, in return, he offered newsworthy nuggets for my Crime Buster column. I didn't agree with those who sneeringly termed him as 'nothing but a spieler', but I had to concur with the general condemnation of his premises. A noxious grey/brown substance dribbled down the stone steps leading to the front door. "Come in," he said. "Don't mind that, we've got a problem with the khazi." We went through the bar where a jar of pickled eggs, last seen in a laboratory, vied for attention alongside a display cabinet of Cornish pasties which had curled up in fright.

Once settled in his back office, he caressed his tumbler of Scotch, took a slug, and said, expansively: "What can I do for you?"

"You knew Jimmy Challinor pretty well, didn't you?"

A mat of black curlies protruded from his V-necked sweater and a gold medallion, hanging from a chain once used to fetter convicts, swung hypnotically every time he moved. Suddenly, he leaned forward. "Look," he said, in a guarded tone, even though no-one else was in the room. "This is off the record. Agreed?" I nodded.

"Okay. I keep reading how popular he was. Cheeky chappie and all that. Truth is, Jimmy was a little shit. Him and Myra were in one of those homes when they were kids. I lived up the road, and she was always coming to me, crying. Full of bruises and worse. If it weren't the wardens, it was Jimmy. Yeah."

Jez rated himself as a hard case. As evidence, he had a brutal, whisky-blotched face and a police record. Section 47 assault, bootleg booze, illegal gambling, the usual stuff. But, flipping over the pages of Myra's history, he revealed his marshmallow centre. "Only 14 she was when they kicked her out. Boys and Girls Welfare Society, my arse." Another swig of Scotch. "Near the end of the war. We'd been bombed."

"What happened to her?"

Jez leered. "How does a nice-looking young bird earn a few pennies? Loads of soldiers around. Jimmy pimped for her, even after they were married. He never made much money as a player, and what he had he gambled away. When his career went down the pan he was in here all the time, talking the talk, cadging drinks. Don't know how she put up with it."

Sly, Jez. Trying to present Myra as the hard done to widow. He knew differently. She was a tough cookie, manipulative, I felt certain. Eventually, he stood up, ushered me to the door. "Come back anytime, have a drink and a snack." No chance, I thought, mindful of the fare on offer.

The Ford Pop was destined for the scrapyard under the new Ministry of Transport tests, but it got me home. "Your phone's been ringing all day," said Joe, a mite peevishly. "You need one of those new-fangled answering machines." Just at that moment it trilled again - Fred at the news desk. "We've had a tip-off that Challinor was selling fake World Cup match tickets. Check it out."

For the next 48 hours I worked the phone hard with little progress. As a last resort, I called Jez. "Yeah," he admitted. "He tried it on here, but priced them way too high. Greedy bastard." His smoker's cough interrupted. "Got to go," he croaked and the line went dead. But I wasn't so easily dismissed. Jez knew I could grass him up for various breaches of the licensing and gaming laws, enough to get The Peacock closed down, if only temporarily. With a little prodding he would gift me a story. An hour later I was at the club, full of hod carriers and brickies from nearby building sites swilling weak ale and watered down whisky, relabelled 'The McSporran – A Unique Blend'. Jez had swapped his usual rig of sweater and slacks for a garish Hawaii type shirt and flared chinos.

I made it simple.

"Jimmy couldn't sell the tickets but refurbished his house. All the latest gear. So what was he into?" He shifted in his chair, and pushed a glass of evil looking liquid towards me. "Good health." I waited.

You had to be patient with someone like Jez. Shifty, he leaked his secrets like a dripping tap. His tale took some time, punctuated as it was with regular pauses, to drink, to kill itches on various parts of his anatomy, or simply for dramatic effect. He had the mobile features worthy of a silent movie actor, thick eyebrows rising and falling, pulpy lips quivering in disgust whenever he spoke Jimmy's name. The office grew clammy, the multi-coloured shirt failed to hide the sweat stains under his armpits, but, eventually, he got to the meat of it.

"Think about it son," he said. "Forged match tickets. Fakes. Jimmy was working with a big-time mob. In the printing business. But the tickets were just a sideline, pocket money. What they were really into was patriotic stuff, copying Her Majesty's phizog onto sheets of paper to distribute to the general public."

"Jesus. Counterfeiting."

"Big-time," confirmed Jez. "All stacked up in a warehouse. Not far from where they found him. And all ready to go as soon as they organised their team of pushers. In the meantime, they gave our Jimmy the job of nightwatchman. Idiots. I wouldn't have left him with a bag of frozen peas. And guess what?" Pause. Glass hovering around his mouth. He was drinking long and hard and fixed me with red-rimmed darts which once were eyes. I remained mute, appreciating how much he preferred to answer his own questions.

"One night the whole stash disappears, about a

million quid's worth face value. Apparently, he'd been shaving bits off before then. Might have got away with it but he had to have it all. Like I've said, a greedy swine. And then he comes in here, stoned out of his head, buying rounds like he's won the pools.

"Course, the boys are onto him like a shot and, what I've heard - only rumour, mind you - is they're giving him a touch of cosmetic surgery, asking him where he's hidden it and all of a sudden he snuffs it." Pause, a smile, a scratch. "I think they forgot he had a weak ticker."

Halfway through the door, I glimpsed a couple of expensive looking suitcases in the corner. Jez had his feet up on the desk, grinning. Holiday mode.

"Costa del Sol, Jez?"

"Nah, that's where all the villains go. We've got somewhere classy in mind."

"We?"

"Yeah."

*****

We closed the Acropolis for the last time in mid-August without any regrets. World Cup fever was over, business slack, Britain close to bankruptcy, and the city choking in its own detritus. Joe and Gloria went first, by ferry to Holland and then by train through Europe and into Greece. I stayed in various seaside B and Bs before flying out. Soon, we were scoffing spanakopita in a cafe in the Crete capital, Heraklion, having settled on the purchase of a remote hillside villa, close to the fishing village of Matala and the 2000 years-old Minoan ruins on the south coast. Gloria fancied the spot because of a story about a Greek god. "It was there that Zeus transformed himself into a white bull to seduce a princess called Europa," she said.

Exchanging our cut of the counterfeit banknotes into genuine cash hadn't been easy, but Joe was a born entrepreneur - and a dark horse who had served in the Special Forces during WW2. An old comrade in arms introduced him to a bent financier in Rotterdam and, via a convoluted series of transactions involving a diamond merchant in Antwerp, our £100,000 of fakes earned £20,000 in real ones, a fortune In those days. The property, with terraces and a small olive grove, cost under £2,000, and we split the rest. Joe wanted to open a hotel. "Tourism is the future here," he said. "Gloria's new friends are the pioneers."

Gloria was in her element, either debating The Meaning Of It All with the band of international hippies who had invaded the sandy cove at the foot of our hill or exploring the sacred cave of Kanares, which was an archaeologist's treasure trove. Sometimes she went to all-night raves on the beach, dancing naked around a fire. Joe enjoyed reminiscing about wartime exploits with a tanned, pony-tailed German named Eric, an ex-paratrooper who had fought in Crete and had returned to open a bar.

"What will you do with your money," Joe asked me one evening. "You can't leave it hanging about in the bank."

"I'm thinking about it. What will you call your hotel?"

"The Golden Fry, what else?"

One morning, a snazzy sports car rolled up. Myra climbed out, elegantly, despite the deep bucket passenger seat. White two-piece suit, a wide-brimmed hat shading her face. The driver, a young-looking Greek, stayed put, smoking. Menthol, I bet.

"Where's Jez," I asked.

She avoided my stare. "Haven't seen much of him lately. I've got the feeling he wants to go back." She glanced at the driver. "No arguments from me." They had tried Ibiza first, only to come second best in a drugs swindle and so followed us to Crete, needing somewhere quieter and cheaper. Obviously, that hadn't worked either.

We drank beer, chilled in a nearby natural spring, chewed crusty bread and sucked olives. Myra said little, she had just fancied some cooler air, an excursion into the hills for a tonic. Life in their coastal villa got dull. We heard her and the young man laughing as he eased the motor down the slope. "Some woman, that," said Joe. Gloria sniffed haughtily. "You did well," she told me that night when, inevitably, Myra cropped up in the conversation. "Tell us again what happened. I love hearing it, just picturing her face."

"It's boring," I groaned. But she pressed.

It's some years ago now, so forgive me if I'm short

on the detail.

After leaving Jez at the club, I drove to Myra's and waited in the Pop, reading a paper. An hour or so passed, and I was ready to admit my hunch was wrong. Then a red Ford Cortina pulled up, Jez at the wheel. Myra got out, pushed the front gate open, and disappeared around the back. Minutes later Jez followed, lugging the suitcases

They were in the greenhouse, doubtless sweating, and too occupied to spot me, until I startled them by banging on one of the panes of glass, cracking it. Jez wheeled around, right arm extended, something blue and metallic in his hand. "Oh," he said. "It's you." He pointed the revolver at my head, laughing. A Colt Pocket 32 I reckoned. Small, but lethal at point blank range and for a moment the barrel was six inches from my frontal lobe only for Jez to gently lower his arm.

Myra made a grab for the gun, screaming: "I'll do it if you haven't got the guts!" But Jez gently pushed her away. He was a sleaze-ball but not a killer. Not a face to face one, anyway.

Stacks of banknotes were piled on a potting bench, beside a row of empty Tupperware boxes. Myra shrugged, resignedly. "He hid them in his tomato compost bags. No-one would have guessed but thankfully he had a big mouth, especially in drink."

Jez elaborated for me. "Spilled it all that night when he made a nuisance of himself in the club. I promised to keep quiet in return for a small fee.

Huh. 'Course, then the boys got hold of him and, well, you've probably guessed the rest." Although a fool, Jimmy was tougher than he seemed. He refused to confess but, just as his torturers were about to step up their interrogation, his heart surrendered and the secret of the hiding place was left in the grubby mitts of the proprietor of the Peacock Club. Along with Jimmy's wife.

Jimmy had grown his tomato plants up strings attached to the greenhouse's roof. The fruit had withered. Jez picked one, green with yellow spots, examined it and chucked it away. "Poor old Jimmy. But there is always a bright side, isn't there darling?" chucking Myra under the chin. He switched to me. "And, I suppose we'll have to buy your co-operation. Am I right, son?" A blatant bribe but a big improvement on a bullet. But I made them wait. Pause. Scratch. Then…

"Deal."

Gloria was right. Myra had rated me one of life's innocents. Her disbelieving face was something to behold.

Jez offered me 10 percent, kindly explaining: "Find the right guys to deal it for you and you'll end up with plenty. For your purposes. I need more, Myra isn't cheap to maintain." He looked at her, laughed his gruff laugh. She leaned against the greenhouse door, smoking, sulking. "Oh yeah," she said, venom twisting her face. "It'll cost him."

We sifted the piles of fivers and tenners, he even joked about it. "One for you, 10 for me", and Joe and Gloria offered little resistance when, back at the cafe, I slapped a compost bag onto a table, 'fruit' tumbling out of it, and suggested a new life, somewhere more suitable for debates on Greek philosophy.

I never fully understood why Jez let me in on it. True, he couldn't keep a secret, but there was something more. Not trusting Myra, maybe he needed me as back-up. But, in that case, he was more perceptive than I'd ever imagined, discerning the something in me, the dark side that I thought I'd kept under wraps. Anyway, judge me as you will. As Gloria commented one ouzo-fired evening. "Good and bad – they twist around each other like grapevines. Discuss."

****

I left Crete the following Easter. The hillside was still tinged with its winter green, the newly whitewashed house sparkled and a fresh breeze whipped up white horses as the tide powered into the bay.

Gloria hugged me, whispering something in Greek which I didn't comprehend. Joe told me to watch my step.

The cafe was boarded up and gloomy, but nothing that a lick of paint wouldn't fix. And, at least, it was mine. I replaced the fading Acropolis sign with one advertising 'Zeus Private Inquiry Agency'. The Peacock's old number was still operative. A throaty voice, thick with nicotine answered.

"Oh, it's you. Come around for a spot of lunch.

Scotch and a pasty." Pause. "On the house."

THE LOCAL RAG

(an essay on local newspapers, published in History UK Magazine)

T HE Local Rag has been defined as a 'local newspaper, especially one regarded as lacking quality or substance'. Unfortunately, this demeaning description, first used in the mid-19th century in The London Magazine, came to be applied to almost every weekly paper from then on. Yet, no matter what the standard of journalism, the Local Rag developed into one of the mainstays of British culture, particularly in the 20th century before the advent of new technology.

Perhaps its high point was in the post WW2 decades when the retail economy expanded and, with no competition from TV and radio, newspaper advertising grew exponentially.

The Local Rag of the 1950s-1960s was extremely popular, and therefore, equally influential. For example, in the small, historic town of Knutsford, the 'Guardian' enjoyed saturation coverage, with 3000 paid-for copies flying over the newsagents' counters each Thursday. Part of the Warrington Guardian series, which had a dozen offices dribbling across the broad chest of Cheshire, this particular recorder of the local scene had changed little since its emergence in the early part of the 20th century. It was a broadsheet paper, awkward to fold or open, with its front and back pages obliterated by large 'Display' adverts. Several pages inside carried the 'Classifieds' and a reader had to delve deep inside to find the news, most of which stemmed from council meetings, court hearings, and the comings and goings of the town's organisations such as the Women's Institute, the Round Table, and the Parochial Church Councils.

Typical of Local Rag reporting is this extract from a North Wales weekly in mid-1964.

'Easter Bonnets at the W.I' was the engaging headline. It continued: *'The President welcomed members, and Miss Horner from the electricity board gave a demonstration of cooking by electricity. For the monthly competition members had been asked to trim an Easter bonnet....'*

The most read page in any weekly of that era featured the Births, Marriages and Deaths column, accompanied by the 'obits' – fulsome funeral reports which included lengthy lists of mourners and floral tributes. But, overall, if you wanted to know what was going on in your town you had to buy The Local Rag. It informed, sparked debate, and thereby underpinned democracy. (Mahatma Gandhi said a newspaper was the first thing he would set up in any village in India).

Britain's first weekly appeared in the early 18th century and they increased quickly. By 1750 many towns had one. Aberdeen had the Press and Journal, Newcastle the Courant, Derby the Mercury, and Canterbury the Kentish Weekly Post. They carried district news but also reports of national and international import along with fire-brand leading articles. Two hundred years later, the emphasis was unashamedly local, with non-confrontational editorials. However, the Local Rag remained highly influential. If you wanted publicity for a jumble sale or a summer garden fete, or simply to find out if the council were planning a new road through your garden, it was the only reliable source.

As well as peeking into the pages of the Local Rag, we can also take a tour of its post-war HQ. Take the Guardian office in Knutsford - a late Victorian era building with a front counter for general enquiries, a small cubicle for the advertising manager, and the newsroom where the editor and two reporters hammered away at huge, pre-war typewriters made by Imperial and Underwood. The clatter of these machines combined with the shrill ring of three black bakelite General Post Office phones, each weighing 1.6 kg – although by then the GPO had introduced the 'Modern Telephone' which was lighter with a choice of seven colours, but retained a rotary dial and coiled handset cord. Yellowing net curtains covered the office windows and cigarette smoke mingled with the dust which danced in the air.

The reporters, aged 16 and 20, used biros to fill their spiral backed notebooks with Pitman's shorthand. Weekly newspapers were a nursery for journalists with school-leavers taken on if they were the right material, although there was a heavy bias in favour of males. In the mid-1960s a budding reporter needed at least 3 GCE O levels including, of course, English, a lively mind, and the willingness to work long hours for low wages. The starting rate for such a novice was £6-£8 a week. After a six months' probation period he had to sign a three years' indentureship – which also needed the approval of his parents – during which he improved his shorthand speed to at least 100 words per minute and learned other journalistic essentials such as local government practice and law.

The office on the main street was a hub of activity. Sometimes a queue formed of people wanting to place adverts, to order photographs which had appeared in that week's edition, to submit reports or to complain that their name was missing from the list of mourners at a funeral. Local traders, publicans and councillors came in merely for a chat over a mug of coffee.

In fact, the theory that The Local Rag lacked quality or substance misses the point. It may sometimes have appeared mundane, trivial and even naïve, but as Gandhi insisted, it was the community's Information Desk and an essential, integral feature of local life.

SCENT OF INDIA

*(A personal history published in the Families
of British India Society quarterly Journal)*

MY first visit to India changed my life.
January 1996. I was a 48 years-old
grandad, accompanied by a 21 years-old
newspaper colleague, fresh out of uni. I'd promised
his mum to take good care of him. Of course, he
ended up having to look after me.

We were there to cover the cricket World Cup,
a tournament lasting almost two months. I
had misgivings prompted by others with some
experience of the sub-continent. Take a mosquito
net, your own food etc. Those qualms were
accentuated by something I ate or drank on the
flight and, in transit at Dubai, I was terribly sick.
By the time we landed at Mumbai, I was reeling.

Fortunately, we got through customs without too
much bother and went out of the airport to grab
a cab – straight into the blinding heat and glare of
the mid-day sun. And the smell I'd been warned
about, a musty, stale version of petrichor.

Yet in the back of the white Ambassador grunting

its way through the Mumbai traffic towards Nariman Point I suddenly felt much better. And the strangest of feelings, a familiarity, almost as though I'd been there before, that I was home. It grew stronger.

A few months later, back in the UK, my father showed me a letter he'd received from a long forgotten niece asking for information to help with the family history she was compiling. In it she mentioned an ancestor who had once lived in an orphanage in Madras. I was nearly sick again, this time with excitement.

No-one in my family had ever said anything remotely connected with India. Apologies – Dad had informed us that he hated curry. Otherwise, nothing. Yet this letter triggered years of research which revealed that we had been part, admittedly a tiny part, of British India. Perhaps, more significantly, it welded for my wife and me a love of India, a respect for its culture (albeit with some reservations), and a fragile appreciation of its problems. Now, so many years on, we smell India wherever we may be, a busy city street (spice restaurants aplenty so that's understandable!) but perhaps also on a Scottish hillside, full of bell heather and cotton grass.

Anyway, one of the things we quickly discovered about my Indian heritage was that my gx3 grandfather sailed out to Madras in 1813 as a new recruit of the East India Co Army. He was 20 years-old Thomas Avery, born in Benson, a village just across the River Thames from the historic market town of Wallingford and his ship was Rose (not 'The Rose' just 'Rose'), captained by James Sandilands.

Rose was a new ship, owned by a consortium and on only her second voyage. Weighing 955 tons, she had three decks offering ample head height of six feet two inches and carried hundreds of soldiers, most from Ireland, then Europe's poorest nation. She was part of a convoy protected by frigates - Napoleon's navy was still intent on wreaking havoc - and slipped her moorings in the Solent on a cold January morning, arriving in the baking mid-summer heat of Madras over five months later in early July. On the way she called in at Cape Town having passed St Helena.

Thomas had described himself as a clerk when he enlisted under a Captain Grainger and it's possible that he had worked with his father Arthur Avery who was a tithe collector in Oxfordshire and what now would be described as West London. In India Thomas began as a matross, the bottom rung, with the Madras Horse Artillery.

I've often wondered about Thomas's reaction on seeing Madras for the first time after his upbringing on the banks of the Thames.

As there was no harbour, ships had to moor two or three miles from the shore so he would have had a distant view, although a clear one. First the Coromandel coast, dull and flat, hardly inviting. Then the beach, much more interesting, with its long, lofty line of buildings, the Custom House, Supreme Court, and Offices of the Houses of Agencies on the right; Fort St George on the left, resplendent with flagstaff. Further back a fascinating skyline, the roofs of public buildings, flags representing Hindu gods, towers and spires of Madras's proliferating number of churches (Armenian, Roman Catholic, Scottish and English), the minarets of mosques, and the brass and copper Hindu pagodas glinting in the sun.

Close up, Thomas would have also seen the red dirt roads of Black Town, the commercial centre of Madras, busy with four wheeled gigs and bullock drawn carts, and then the tree-lined avenues of elegant mansions extending further south towards the former Portuguese citadel of St Thomas Mount. Black Town, asserted the missionary Elijah Hoole, was 'unsuitable for European habitation'. The drainage was poor and you had to hold your nose against the 'foul smells' emitting from certain areas.

But, even before reaching dry land, Thomas had to undergo a tricky journey through the surf. For this he relied on the Madras kariears (beachmen) who negotiated a passage between ship and shore through three sets of waves which often rose more than six feet, threatening to topple their masoola boats, constructed from wood and coir. These vessels needed 10 pairs of hands, eight rowing and keeping time with a shanty type song, one at the tiller, and a boy to do the bailing out and were each accompanied by a catamaran (from the Tamil kathamaram – *katha* meaning tied and *maram* wood) which had a crew of two or three who had to be of the same caste as those in the masoola.

These indigenous seamen were all Roman Catholics having been converted from Hinduism or Islam by the original Portuguese settlers. They lived in a village named Royapooram, vaguely to the north of Black Town and, although lowly paid, raised enough money to build their own church there. As well as passengers, they carried important and sometimes confidential documents to and from the ships, wrapping them in waxed cloth and pushing them into their cylindrical caps, made from palm leaves. It's clear they were loyal and trustworthy as well as being brave and highly skilled. Invariably passengers in the masoolas got soaked. Even when they hit the beach, the water was still knee deep and ladies, dignatories and the less mobile had to complete the passage in rather undignified style on the backs of the kariears.

(When my wife and I first arrived in Chennai, as it was re-named in the 1990s, we too got drenched. It was November and a late monsoon flooded the city so badly that loudspeaker announcements warned constantly about the dangers of infection from rat urine).

Initially, I assumed Thomas must have suffered from the heat and smell of Madras, but Elijah Hoole who arrived there in 1820, made me briefly re-consider. He stated: "Like the generality of persons on their first arrival I did not think the heat worth noticing. The clear and constant shining of the sun, the lightness and freedom of the air..."

Hmm. Slightly romantic, I fear. 'The constant shining of the sun' was a death trap for many Europeans in India.

Thomas' early impressions of the city might have been of a busy, prosperous place (although corruption and poverty lay just under the surface). Black Town was walled to the north and west, protected to the south by the fort and to the east by the ocean, and had five gates leading to a criss-cross of streets accommodating public offices, shops, bazaars and taverns. Only a few Europeans lived there, although some of European descent mixed with the mass of Armenians and natives speaking in Tamil, Telegoo and Hindi.

'It is worth noting," reported Missionary Hoole, "that in this populous, central place there are no Jews.'

While there were military barracks inside the fort, I believe Thomas was quartered in barracks several miles to the south near St Thomas Mount and where the St Thomas Garrison Church was erected. It was at this church that my wife and I knocked down one of those brick walls which all family historians collide with at some stage of their research.

*****

It was 2008, terrorists were attacking Mumbai and Chennai was knee deep in flood water and rat pee. We were hoping to get to the church to view the BMD registers, aiming to find records of Thomas' three marriages, first to an Elizabeth Brown, then a Charlotte Hobeau, and finally to Julia Wardle, all between 1819 and 1831. The one which intrigued us most was Charlotte.

'Hobeau', a curious surname, but one which we had seen on an India Office document in the British Library and, so, surely correct although for years we had failed to trace her antecedents or even to garner enough clues to hazard a guess. The original marriage register, held at the church, might help, we thought. But how to reach it, marooned as we were. We hung around for a couple of days, glued to the TV as the terrible events in Mumbai unfolded, and then, gloriously, the sun emerged. Trains were still being halted, one bus was stuck in a water-filled underpass, but for once forsaking public transport we engaged a car and driver and, slowly, carefully, he wound his way south.

At the church we found the pastor, the tall, graceful, silver-haired Prince Pookanamar who sat us down in his little office and served us cans of Cola. Half an hour later he led us into the church, sat us down again, opened a chest of drawers and pulled out a huge red hide-bound book blowing decades of dust off it as he set it down on a table in front of us. Within minutes we had found

Thomas's marriage to Charlotte. But not Hobeau. Hobson. The mistake was easy to understand, seeing the handwriting, how the name had been transformed by a clerk and remitted to the East India Co offices in London. But we checked and re-checked, together and individually, and it was definitely Hobson. Which nullified several years of searching for the Hobeau link – a false trail which led back to the Pilgrim Fathers in New England.

Thomas and Charlotte married at St Thomas Mount in 1824. She was his second wife, he was her third husband. Birth, marriage and death swarmed like flies in those times. They had several children, two of which survived into adulthood. One was my great great grandmother, Amelia. The other, Edmund who helped to spread the telegraph network in India. Their stories are common enough within the annals of British India, but, I feel, worth summarising, perhaps in a future issue.

Charlotte died in 1831 aged 30 and was buried in AGRAM (Army Grounds And Maidan), Bangalore, an old and fascinating cemetery hidden behind military lines and inaccessible to the public without specific permission from the authorities, which, appreciating Indian bureaucracy, would have caused problems. However, we were helped by a remarkable man, Admiral O S Dawson, former Chief of the Indian Navy, who met us, led us serenely past a sign saying: 'Air Force Officers' Mess', armed sentries snapping to attention, and organised a platoon of soldiers to machete their way through the jungle which had enveloped the long dis-used site. And, although many of the memorial stones were fragmented, hidden by vines and the inscriptions indecipherable, we found her grave, standing quite proud in a little sun rippled clearing. A tear-jerking moment.

Charlotte's grave in AGRAM cemetery, Bangalore
Reverting to Thomas Avery, he made his way in the army finishing as a Quarter-Master Sergeant in the Madras Horse Artillery, stationed at Bangalore

Fort where he died in 1833 aged 40 after serving for 20 continuous years, an unusually long spell in the south of India. Sadly, the cemetery in the fort was demolished some years ago, there is no record of him being in AGRAM and so we don't know where he was buried.

Apart from muster rolls, it is difficult to describe his army service. It's possible that he saw action in the Third Anglo-Maratha War in which Madras troops fought bands of marauding Pindaris on the Coromandel coast. As he was stationed at Bangalore for periods it is also possible that he knew Seringapatnam, the battle scarred fort of Sultan Tipu, the Tiger of Mysore whose war against the British ended in 1799 when his base was bombarded and then ravaged. There is a lane there that heads towards a picturesque spot on the Cauvery River close to a military cemetery, and where a former East India Army HQ still stands. We have walked that lane many times and it would be nice to think that we have trod in his footsteps. Or the hooves of his horse.

Army enlistment forms identify him as physically average for that period, five feet six inches tall, with blue eyes, brown hair and an open complexion - a bit like my father whose name was Thomas Avery Evans but who knew nothing of the Indian connection. Other than that, we know little about him. Just another soldier.

Except he made a stash of money. Because he died intestate, probably suddenly from cholera, his estate was administered by the Supreme Court and, as such, publicised. It amounted to 3,090 Madras rupees (the city minted its own silver coin). Trying to covert that to sterling values is a minefield, but my estimation is about £300 which in that era would have bought him a London house with change. The court divided the estate between his family and re-allocated it as various members of the family bit the dust. Eventually his daughter Amelia, my great great grandmother, received half. Perhaps that persuaded her and her husband – another East India Co soldier – to swap the heat and dust of Madras for the cold and damp of a Lancashire mill town. In hindsight, a bad choice. For her. But, for me, well thank you Amelia. I couldn't have made it without you.

THE SQUEEZE

*(Entry for a competition with the prompt 'squeeze',
max 250 words. Hometown – good and bad)*

H E reached down for the little boy's hand, grasped it to reassure him.

'Ouch!'

'Oh, sorry Leo. Didn't mean to hurt you.'

Behind them a laugh. Slim blonde. Mum.

'Great Grandad doesn't know his own strength.'

Ambling through warm, dusky streets. Back in Hometown. Historic, quaint, so they said. Fine place to bring up a family. Now, maybe. But not before. The house that wasn't a home, the street fights, the glinting blades. He grimaced. Now everything was soft. The lighting. The padded indulgence oozing from open cafe bar windows. The life.

'Why are you so tall?' Leo asked, squinting upwards.

'I eat my greens.'

'What's greens?'

Crowding onto the narrow pavement to escape a menacing, rumbling convoy of black SUVs.

Turning to his grand-daughter. 'Is it always like this?'

She smiled.'I'd love a Discovery.'

'I remember seeing a horse and cart coming through here. The rag 'n bone man.'

'Seventy years ago, Grandad.'

His lifetime. A council estate wannabe who had balanced precariously on the rim of respectability. He fell on the right side but it was close and, in the growing gloom, he spied yesteryear's scowling phantoms flitting around the Georgian stone, the Victorian brick and the modern ersatz. An ambush? The old fear iced him.

Leo wriggled, tried to pull away. 'Mummy, tell Great Grandad to stop squeezing - he's hurting me again.'

'Grandad, you've got to be more careful.'

Yes. He had.

DAISY UP THE AMAZON

(Entered in a competition for bizarre
travel tales – max words 4,000)

I T was at the Meeting Of The Waters that Daisy realised her life – at least what was left of it – was missing something. Here, where the sandy coloured Amazon and the black Rio Negro collided but refused to mix, she felt bewildered, vaguely apprehensive but curious, wondering what might lie below the surface. Two months earlier she had given a talk on jam-making to her Women's Institute colleagues. Now, shrouded by creeping, claustrophobic jungle and mesmerised by the vessel's passage through this mysterious environment, she felt her lungs tightening, her pulse accelerating, and reacted suddenly when something tugged at her elbow.

"Yes, what? Oh, Charles. You were saying?"

Her husband stood there, an anxious smile between his blue, brass buttoned blazer and jauntily perched Panama hat.

"You were well away there, Daisy."

"Oh, sorry. But isn't it remarkable? Two entirely different colours of water." She paused for a moment, eyes screwed up, pulling her artist's palette into mind. "One half of the boat in Payne's Grey, the other half in Raw Sienna. How can they stay separate?"

"Beats me," he said, shrugging his shoulders. "I'm no scientist. Here's the purser. You can interrogate him. I'm thirsty." He moved off towards the first-class lounge bar.

All 210 of the SS Shirley's passengers were on deck to witness the phenomenon, switching rapidly and noisily from port to starboard, starboard to port. The purser Mr Slattery had given up trying to control the sudden surges and had quickly grown exasperated at some of the questions thrown at him.

"Is it something to do with the moon and gravity?" was the last one.

He wiped his brow with a hand towel, excused himself and, seeing Charles heading for the bar, quick-stepped after him only to be halted by Mrs Warren, whom he considered polite, approachable, perhaps even a little vulnerable and therefore worthy of his attention. At least for a few seconds.

"Good afternoon Mr Slattery. I wonder – can you explain? Briefly, of course. I don't want to delay you, especially if you're meeting Charles for a drink."

Slattery did not detect any hint of sarcasm, although it must be said, he wasn't the most perceptive of souls, especially as this trip was his swansong on the Liverpool-Manaus run and, as he told the ship's mate, he couldn't give 'a monkey's', adding: "You can stick the Amazon. Give me the Mersey fog any day."

He settled in front of her. "Certainly, Mrs Warren." He was stocky with a drinker's florid face. Sweat flooded down it.

"The different colours are something to do with sediment. The Negro originates from Colombia, the Amazon from the Andes." He anticipated the next query. "But why don't they blend together, well it's a mystery, ma'am. One of the many mysteries around here."

"Mysteries?"

Slattery hesitated. "Well, yes. Water spirits and strange goings on but it's mostly talk – for the tourists, y'know."

"Mostly, Mr Slattery?"

Again he seemed reluctant to answer. "M'am, I wouldn't worry about it. Now I must get on. Excuse me."

Accepting her muted 'Thank you' with a token salute he rolled away with the gait of a seaman who had long experience of much rougher waters, mainly with the Atlantic convoys in WW2. Now, after a decade of service with Brent's Line cruises, he'd had enough. Daisy watched him glance up and down the deck before pushing open the bar door.

The Shirley was making slow, deliberate progress. Gradually as they steamed west the river colours did become one. She plucked at her silver cigarette case.

"May I?" The voice was light, soft. An antidote to the raucous laughs from the stern where a canvas 'swimming pool' had been set up and to the screeching of parakeets, monkeys and other inhabitants of the Brazilian jungle.

Dr Ortega flicked a lighter. She wished it were someone else but his manners were impeccable. So she said: "That's very kind," leaned forward and pushed the cigarette into the flame. Then realigned her body into cocktail party mode, cigarette held high in the left hand, exhaling the smoke over the rail so that it plumed back along the dazzling white painted hull.

"The objective," they told her at finishing school, "is to look composed and in control." All those years ago. And, now, when it mattered not one whit, she still did it, automatically, particularly when surprised. Like a defence mechanism.

"I could not help overhearing," Ortega said. "Perhaps I can satisfy your curiosity."

She frowned.

"I mean the Meeting Of The Waters. Why it is so."

A rare hint of breeze ruffled Daisy's Mexican print dress. She palmed it down, noting Ortega's glance.

"Such vibrant colours," he said. "Colours of

Amazonia. Many ladies on board are positively dull by comparison."

"Oh, I wouldn't say that, Doctor Ortega. Indeed, I feel that perhaps it's too gaudy - but you were saying…"

Daisy cursed herself. Charles had urged her to buy it. "It's a chance to break the mould! No more twin set and pearls for my Daisy." Eventually she had no choice. He came home one evening, reeking of alcohol, a large box under his arm. When she ignored it, carried on writing her monthly WI President's report, he pulled the box apart and spread the dress over the back of the sofa.

Typical Charles. Instead of facing the reality and learning to live with it he wasted their time on diversionary fripperies. Oh yes, a sunshine dress. That would take her mind off everything. And when she questioned its suitability for the county WI's annual meeting and the singing of Jerusalem, he raised a finger and said playfully: "Quite so my dear. But it will look super up the Amazon."

And with that he waved an envelope in front of her. "And that's where we're headed. Six weeks luxury cruise! I've got the tickets. Portugal, the Caribbean, and then…."

At that point Daisy had burst into tears, recovering quickly. "Sorry, just shock, such a wonderful surprise." Later, when he had gone to the Hare and Hounds for a 'quick snifter' she sat on the edge of their bed sobbing.

Ortega broke into her thoughts. "Mrs Warren, my

apologies. I'm intruding."

"No, no, please." Embarrassed. Her lifelong tendency to drift away was getting worse. Soon people would start to think of her as rude or dismissive. She would hate that but had recognised recently she was caring a little less about how others viewed her.

Ortega was tall, slim, a good-looking man with a high forehead, hair slicked back. He reminded her of Basil Rathbone, the actor who had played Sherlock Holmes although his colour was different, olive, akin to the now blended river waters. His voice was reedy yet somehow engaging.

"I overheard the purser saying about the different sediments, and who am I to argue with such an illustrious personage. But the temperatures and flow of the rivers are the significant factors – they are at odds with one another." Ortega smiled. "And they refuse to come together. You might say like an unconsummated marriage."

Provocative. But, if he had hoped for a typical English lady's blush, he had picked the wrong one. Despite her current fallibility, Daisy Warren was built of sterner stuff. Had to be, married to Charles. She inhaled, pursed her lips into an oval and blew it out.

"Well, Doctor. That's fascinating. I must tell my husband. Excuse me." And with that she threw the cigarette into the Amazon - or was it the Negro? - turned and walked away, not too quickly, feeling his eyes on her.

"He gives me the creeps, Charles," she said, accepting a large gin.

"I'm sure he didn't mean anything by it, dear. Seems quite a charmer."

Hmm, she thought. Charles all over, determined to walk on the sunny side of the street, afraid of shadows. Wouldn't even accompany her to the hospital, fearing the verdict. Unlike Slattery who had sneered at her first mention of Ortega. "Bloody doctor," he muttered unashamedly. "Comes over smooth and sophisticated but I wouldn't trust him with my..." Charles had turned to give him a warning look. "Apologies ma 'am. Wouldn't normally speak ill of anyone but he raises my hackles."

*****

Next day, the SS Shirley berthed and disgorged its passengers into the streets of Manaus, free to do as they pleased – except, insisted the purser, not to talk to strangers and to be back on board by five o'clock.

"You don't want to be walking around here in the dark."

"Like being at school," said Charles.

"Yes, or on parole from prison," said Daisy, offhand. He laughed, half-heartedly. Nowadays, with Daisy, he was never sure of anything. She had changed. Or maybe not. Perhaps she had always been like this, sometimes immersed in her own thoughts, sometimes edgy. Not that he would ever say anything. Too late, now.

They joined a group led by a tour guide.

"Manaus," she bleated. "The City of Dreams."

"Aren't they all?" thought Daisy.

The guide, a 30s something woman in cut-off slacks and a blouse tied at the waist, was getting into full flow as they approached the Opera House. "Once this was a simple tribal village, deep in the jungle. Within a few years it was a city, a rich city. How? Rubber, my friends. Manaus was built on rubber. But then it went into decline. Want to know why? Too many cheques bounced!"

There was laughter but from behind, over her right shoulder, a note of contempt. "Yes, such a good joke, don't you agree, Mrs Warren?"

His eyes gleamed. One, the left, she thought was much darker than the other.

"I suppose she is doing her best to keep everyone entertained," she said, constrained to defend the guide simply because she didn't want to be coerced into agreeing with him. For the second time in 24 hours she felt as though he was attempting to trap her.

Ortega wore a cream linen suit, a light blue shirt with a striped tie. Early fifties, similar to her and Charles. One of the other cruisers had whispered to her early on the voyage: "Not a medical doctor. A professor. Something to do with anthropology. Speaks lots of languages."

Daisy had noticed other women weighing him up from their loungers, spying him from behind their magazines and books as he strolled along the deck.

Ortega doffed his Panama, switched his cane from his left to his right hand and offered her an arm.

"Forgive me if I'm mistaken," he said. "But I believe that you would rather see the real Manaus. Come, let me provide an alternative tour."

Daisy rarely panicked, but this was one of those moments. Her head swivelled, searching for Charles or the purser, anyone she could signal to, use as an excuse to remove herself, but the group were moving away and she knew anyway that by now her husband and Slattery would be sitting in a hotel bar, underneath whirring fans, sipping cold beer, sighing gratefully in the cool air, toasting their escape from the oppressive heat and crowds.

"Please be assured," murmured Ortega. "You will be completely safe. Come, I have a car."

He led her to a white Ambassador taxi, a skinny, high-cheeked man at the wheel. His neck and arms were covered in tattoos. Ortega opened the rear door, she climbed in flattening her dress as she did so and he got in beside her. An hour later they were well away from the city, bumping along a rutted red dirt track, deep jungle pressing in, and Daisy, having long ago accepted her misjudgement, was leaning back, gazing steadfastly out of the window, feeling Ortega's fingernail lightly grazing her wrist. She might easily have moved her hand away. But she didn't.

*****

"This," said Ortega, sweeping his hand in a wide arc, "is the real Manaus."

Daisy blinked. She saw a scattering of huts raised on platforms, smoke rising from the largest. Tribes people went about their business. Or rather, the women did. Some were grinding grain, others tilling their version of a kitchen garden, one had a baby suckling at her bare breast. A group of men sat cross-legged in a semi-circle smoking. Only the children paid her any attention, sneaking up behind her, pulling at her dress, giggling and darting away.

"The real Manaus?" she queried, sceptically, the sensuality of Ortega's fingertips long faded. Now she was tired and clammy in need of a shower, her chest tight, breathing laboured. She thought longingly of the Shirley's salon.

"Well, yes and no," he replied with a snigger. "I admit that now this place is part of the claptrap they feed to the tourists. But once this was a genuine tribal settlement. Home to the Manaos."

Ortega's face contorted with anger. "It was their ancestors who slaved away to make the European invaders so immensely wealthy. What did they get in return? The Opera House. As you can see, the Manaos like nothing better than a night at the opera."

As he steered her around the village his tone grew ever more bitter and spiteful. He talked of his parents, his father a Colombian merchant, his mother a tribal woman who had filled him with dire stories of how the true people of the Amazon had been manipulated and abused. The terrible things which happened if they failed to meet their rubber quotas.

"You are not a delicate person," he said. "And so I can tell you. They were treated like animals. Worse. Flogged and tortured. There are reliable accounts that some men were doused in petrol and set alight. Others were forced to watch their wives raped."

Despite the heat, Daisy shuddered. For a few moments Ortegas's eyes burned. She was fascinated by them, the right filled with light, the left jet black, with a diamond tip of light in the centre, drawing her in. She had to pull herself away.

"These people," Ortega continued gesturing towards the huts, "have had to fight hard to keep their heritage. They take money from the tourists, put on an exhibition for the tourists, show them their poisoned arrows, pose for the cameras, but they never forget who they really are. Their beliefs and rituals remain at their very core."

"But it's still not the real Manaus, is it Doctor? You tricked me." Daisy had recovered her equilibrium, showing the resolve that every WI President needed. Ortega muttered something unintelligible and left her standing in a hut doorway while he spoke in a strange language to a tribesman. Returning, he told her: "We must go now."

In the rear of the car, Ortega sat well away from

Daisy, saying little. Exhausted, she dozed until darkness fell and the lights of the city pierced her consciousness. Back on board the Shirley, Slattery complained: "We were looking all over for you, Mrs Warren. Extremely concerned, we were."

"Well, I'm so…"

But Ortega intervened. "My sincere apologies Mr Slattery. I must take full responsibility for the delay. I was so keen to show Mrs Warren the sights that I forgot about your *curfew*. Please forgive me." He bowed to Daisy, tipped his hat to Slattery and Charles, and walked towards his starboard side cabin.

Slattery fumed. "It wasn't a curfew, just a warning about.." But not for the first time in their acquaintanceship, Charles cut him short, determined to avoid a row. He suggested a couple of stiff Martinis before dinner.

"Oh, most certainly," enthused the purser.

"Yes, dear. If we must," said Daisy.

Charles rubbed his hands together. "That's settled then."

He saw her staring at him. He stared back, puzzled.

"Are you alright?" he asked.

"Yes, why?"

"Well, just for a second your left eye changed colour. Black. Completely black."

"Oh, just tiredness, I expect. No need to worry."

Which is what she always said. And which he always accepted without further ado. The real problem was not merely that her left eye had slipped into shadow it was also monitoring things differently. Movement slower, objects rippled by water. But she didn't mention it to Charles. Neither did she show him the peculiar dark lines on her wrist, cross-hatched, just under her skin., like a geometric design waiting to be traced.

*****

Daisy excused herself next day from a trip into the jungle to see what the guide described as the 'genuine thing', jungle life. A headache and a 'dipsy' stomach, she said. Jeeps were laid on. Other passengers trailed around the city again. Charles and Slattery, now thick as thieves, were nowhere to be seen. Daisy, wearing an eyeshade, was relaxing in a deckchair when Ortega's voice roused her. She hadn't seen or heard him approach.

"Good day, Mrs Warren. How are you feeling? I heard you were unwell."

"Oh, nothing serious, I assure you Doctor Ortega."

"Good. In that case perhaps I can persuade you to join me in another little expedition."

Daisy's skin tingled. She pushed up her eyeshade. "I don't think.."

But he interrupted. "Why have you come here?" And before she could reply. "Are you just like all the others, forsaking knowledge for the easy life, unquestioning, following the tour guides like sheep? Come now Mrs Warren. You want more than that, I know you do. Why do you think I have chosen you?"

Astonished by this outburst, Daisy spluttered: "How dare you. You have no right to speak to me like that. I've a good mind to.."

"Tell your husband, yes." Ortega smiled. "Well, do so. But if you change your mind I will be on the quayside at sunset with the car."

He took her hand carefully, brushed the back of it with his lips and let it fall back into her lap. Later, in the cabin, Daisy fell asleep but dreamed she was drowning. She woke up violently, drenched in perspiration, disorientated, a trickle of sticky blood on her palms, pierced by her clenched fingernails. She washed, examined her eyes in the mirror. Clear. The lines on her wrist had faded. Perhaps she had imagined it all. No reason not to go. On the quayside a white Ambassador, engine running, the same driver, and Ortega's cream linen suit leaning against it.

They drove only a little way this time. Ortega in the front passenger seat, Daisy behind, the windows open, the night air laying heavy on them. When they stopped at the edge of jungle, Ortega led the way on foot along a narrow path. Trees whispered, monkeys screeched, bats winged past their heads.

Soon, different sounds. Water lapping against rock – they must be close to the river. Then, chanting, a drumbeat. At the lip of a wide depression in the land, she looked onto a scene which made her laugh. Ortega, a yard or two ahead, swivelled, his face as fierce as the flaming torches which illuminated the hollow. "You laugh!? At our faith?"

"Oh, Doctor. I'm sorry." But she was still giggling. "It's just the contrast between this and jam-making. They'll never believe it."

"I don't understand. But it doesn't matter. Not now. Come."

Dozens of lightly-clad natives stood in a circle around a small hut made of branches and dried grasses. Many held torches, flaring vertically into the stillness. The chanting had stopped, replaced by a murmuring of anticipation. Suddenly, a single shout from inside the hut and then a man burst out, howling in apparent torment. He wore a horned head-dress, anklets of tinkling bells and an ornate mask with huge eyes, one yellow, one black with a frost white pupil.

"Watch now Mrs Warren," said Ortega. "Watch for the Yukuruna."

She sensed his fingers against her wrist. Grazing their patterns. Slowly, carefully for a few seconds then faster and faster as the shaman whirled his magic. When the murmuring of the crowd declined into a low moaning, she shed any lingering concerns. And, after downing a small bowl of a viscous deep red liquid thrust into her hands by Ortega's chauffeur who had suddenly appeared in front of her, she shed her moth-balled Western inhibitions and her Mexican print dress. Charles's dress.

*****

Charles could barely believe what the tour guide Gloria was saying.

"Do they really?" he asked, his whisky rheumy eyes trying to take in her words and her low-cut blouse at the same time.

They and Slattery occupied a corner of the first-class salon. Charles looked over his shoulder in case anyone else was close enough to hear. Satisfied they were safe he urged Gloria to tell him more. Especially the bit about the…

"Oh yes, sex is a big part of it," she said without hesitation, hamming it up as usual. "The shaman calls up the water spirit from where the rivers meet." Her tone changed from matter of fact into a menacing stage whisper, her arms spread out. "He rises from the depths, takes on human form and has his way with any woman he chooses. In front of everyone."

Slattery, whom they thought was dozing, cut in roughly: "Mumbo jumbo, Charles. Take no notice." Gloria crossed her long slim legs and sniffed loudly. She wasn't as dumb as she sometimes led people to believe. And she could handle the purser with ease.

"You're ignorant, Fergus. It's not a physical thing, as such. They regard it as a sacred act, not something disgusting as we would. The spirit imparts wisdom. It's about understanding the inner self. And realising that this life, the now, isn't the be all and end all."

"Yes, of course," said Slattery. Sarcastic.

Charles, normally slow to react, barked: "Shut up Slattery."

But Slattery wasn't finished. "Fact is this spirit can get nasty, can't he Gloria?" goading her. "If he's in a bad mood. People disappear. Or sometimes he just injects them with his poison and he becomes them, or they become him."

Slattery raised his glass. "A toast to the Yukuruna! And let's hope he doesn't strike tonight."

"You've had more than enough, Fergus. Time to call it a day." Gloria spoke soothingly. Helping him to his feet, she steered him to the door, looked back and said: "Goodnight Charles. Sleep well."

He had hoped she would stay. Somehow, being in her company imbued him with a confidence he rarely experienced. She was interesting, sparky, game for a laugh, the perfect companion for a night at the Hare and Hounds while Daisy, well, the Women's Institute's hut where some of her amateurish landscapes hung on the wall was more her scene. But not to think badly of her, not in her present plight.

She wasn't there when he returned to their cabin but, too doused in drink to question why, he tumbled clumsily onto his bunk and lost consciousness. In the morning he woke to find Daisy sat in front of the dressing table, naked, brushing her hair and humming a song he didn't recognise. More a chant. So full of life as though the consultant had got it all wrong. He glimpsed in the mirror her eye - left or right?- in his dulled hungover state he couldn't work it out. But so intensely black. Except for a Polar White nucleus from which a tear swelled, burst and flowed like a river, Payne's Grey and Raw Sienna, down Daisy's face.

◆ ◆ ◆

Cruising the Amazon

HAVE A DRINK
ON ME

*(Long-listed in the Crimebits competition
for the best introduction to a crime novel,
judged by Val McDermid, max words 250 –
published in Crimbebits2 anthology)*

WHAT Abraham Foster could not understand, as a scientist of some repute, was that anyone could mistake a bottle of nitric acid for brandy. Not least his wife who had listened (albeit sullenly) to his constant lectures and warnings about the perils of certain chemicals.

And yet, here she was, explaining in her spidery scribble that it was some sort of accident. Using a pencil and a scrap of notepaper because, of course, her voice had gone. Hard to talk with scorched vocal chords. Sarah was now writhing in agony, wild-eyed, the bedsheets flung aside. The doctor held up a syringe to the light. "Morphine," he said. "Enough?" Abraham enquired.

"More than enough."

Abraham nodded knowingly. Death was inevitable, better that it be pain-free and as quick as possible. He read Sarah's note, shaking his head in apparent disbelief. Curiously, she had dated it, 'Jan 6, 1903' like an epitaph.

He folded it neatly, once, twice, and placed it in his coat pocket. A thin, wrinkled arm clutched his trouser knee. Her mouth opened wide and silent. He extricated himself, pulling the arm away although he would have preferred to fold it, and walked out. She would understand. He was a scientist, not a priest. An hour later, back in his laboratory, he lit the gas lamp to illuminate his workbench and carefully replaced the labels on the bottles.

Brandy, dangerous stuff. In the wrong hands.

BABY FACE

*(Also long-listed for Crimebits and included
in the anthology Crimebits2 – a skeletal
version of 'The Dirt', see 'Notes')*

JOHN DANIEL carried out his first bank raid on October 12, 1973, a day before his 18th birthday. He used a sawn-off shotgun hidden in a rolled-up umbrella, a demand note carefully printed in bold capitals by his mother, one of the new-type plastic shopping bags and a trolley full of bravado.

Daniel was five feet six inches tall in his Cuban heeled boots and wore thick horn-rimmed specs, an orange shirt and a black PVC coat. Carefully positioning the brolly on the counter, he pushed his mum's message under the cashier's window. She read it, smiled, and handed it back. "That's ridiculous – it's not Rag Week is it?" Helen Murray, attractive and recently married, was then five seconds from being blown to Kingdom Come.

Daniel wiggled the brolly so that the twin barrels nosed through the end of it. His finger creased the trigger. He didn't really care about the money. Adrenaline singed his veins, his face pale, mouth curled in anticipation. Helen realised in time, stifled a scream, opened her drawer and handed over stacks of notes. As he nonchalantly strolled out, the stuffed bag swinging gently at his side, umbrella over his shoulder, she vomited violently and forgot to press the alarm button.

A souped up BMW waited impatiently for him, his girl Sassy revving hard, giggling. Next to her a cool chick in cream linen and Belle Cat shades thinking: "Not good enough. Not good enough for my boy."

TRAVELS WITH
KENDO

*(Highly Commended in the Write Time competition
asking for a travel story with a touch of the bizarre,
max 2,000 words – based on a real incident).*

SOMETHING happened that summer. Everything got quicker, more intense. As though the world had skipped a heartbeat.
One social analyst claimed it was the 'end of civilisation'. Cultural progress drowned by a tsunami of materialism and trivia.

1965. Anything goes. Anything can happen. And we're gaily swinging across all three lanes of the north-bound M1 as Kendo nods off.

Circumstantial luck, I think. Shame, though. Only 17 and I have plans.

On the point of crashing through the central barrier and with Dave screaming in his ear, Kendo jerks back to life, WHOAH!, pulls hard on the wheel and steers us onto the hard shoulder.

Nowadays, a mass collision, multiple deaths. But

this Sunday evening 60 years ago, the motorway has long stretches of uninhabited tarmac. No speed restrictions, no uniforms saying 'Breathe into this'.

Joy ride heaven. Unless, like us, you are hitching a lift in a clapped out removals van, two of us squeezed onto the front bench seat next to a crazy drugged up driver.

"Sorry," groans a crestfallen Kendo. "Dropped off. Been on the road for best part of 24 hours, up and down, up and down."

We feel sympathetic, of course. Poor guy. Kendo, dark hair, thick beard, blazing eyes, sparrow chest encased in an old USA Army combat jacket – a dead ringer for Che. Can't help but like him.

And we'd had plenty of warning. When he juddered to a halt on the southern edge of the M1 in response to our outstretched thumbs, Dave asked him: "How far are you going?"

Kendo smiled. A strange faraway sort of smile. "To the edge of the universe, man. All the way."

Now, I'm thinking: 'More like the end of the universe.'

We've had enough. Like, we enjoy a bit of fun but not on The Wheel of Death. There's a slip road just ahead. We walk away. "Bye man." But a hundred yards up the road, I look back, tap Dave on the arm and point. Kendo's motionless, head in his hands.

Dave searches my face. "You've got to be joking."

As we trudge back, Dave muttering: "Jeez, I don't believe we're doing this," Kendo spies us, leaps to his feet, arms wide open. "Hey man, knew you wouldn't leave me. Ah, such love."

On closer inspection, the damaged van doesn't look too bad. Bent bumper, possibly twisted chassis but could survive for another few hours which is all that we need.

Kendo's fitness is more of a concern.

Glancing at me, Dave says: "If it weren't for the insurance, I'd offer to drive."

Kendo looks up, incredulous. "What insurance?"

Silence. Shrugs. A red Mini-Cooper packed with Mods rushes past, leaving insults in its slipstream. Something like: 'Want a tow.' And 'Losers'.

We half-heartedly proffer the obligatory V signs but the Mini has gone, straddling two lanes and wriggling its butt to mock us.

"No worries," says Kendo. "All I need is to stay awake. A couple of these.." – he produces a pair of white pills from his pocket – "and some fresh air. Hey, got an idea."

Twenty minutes later we're on our way again, a soft summer breeze whistling right through the van, the full-length rear doors having been lifted off their stanchions and laid in the back.

"Sort of a wind tunnel," he explains. "Yeah, nothing like the outdoor life, lads! Ha! Ha!", knuckles whitening on the wheel as the benzedrine uppers kick in, nostrils flaring, eyes fixed on a point beyond the horizon.

A sultry cloudy evening turns into a dark, moonless night. We hit the M6 about 10pm with

Ivanhoe, as he calls the vehicle, bucking like a bronco as he double clutches to shift from second to fourth gear - "No third, man, no third."

Dave's suggestion about headlights is sneeringly brushed off.

"Okay, what about sidelights?"

"Sorry, lads. No lights. Unless you've got some candles. Don't worry. Got all your lives in front of you. Shouldn't be worrying about anything." He talks like he is older generation, square, giving us the wisdom, but I guess him to be mid 20s. At this point, he has swivelled at right angles to face us. "Look. You've got to seize every moment."

I think it interesting how he strokes his beard, as though coaxing secretive philosophy from it. But then it strikes me that if his right hand is occupied in that respect and his left is clamped around Dave's shoulder, what about the ...

"Dave! The wheel."

Luckily, in turning so far around, Kendo's foot has divorced the pedal and we've slowed to around 20mph so when we go into the nearside embankment it doesn't hurt too much. Just a bit of a shaking. And one of the doors has slid out somewhere.

We reach the service station nearest our town without further mishaps. Kendo treats us to 'all day breakfasts' – egg, sausage and beans which have stagnated in a heated tray for 15 hours - and we say thanks, great trip, and he hugs us, advises us to get married and have lots of kids, will keep us forever young, and what's life if not one great adventure.

"Memories, boys," he bawls as he drives away. We rush out of the canteen and onto the bridge to watch him and Ivanhoe merge into the night.

*****

Dave is in a wheelchair, according to his daughter Jo-Ro. Paralysed from the waist down after a bad crash on the M6, signs of vascular dementia -'although he's still got most of his wits about him' – and in a nursing home, chucking beakers of orange and tea at the carers.

"He's talked about you so often." - an FB message - "Any chance you can visit?"

We meet up a few weeks later. She is skinny, fair hair, sparkling blue eyes, jeans and leather jacket.

"You're the image of your dad."

"You were really good friends once, weren't you?"

"Yeah. Grew up on the estate, played football, usual thing."

Dave had gone into scaffolding, me into pen-pushing. Hadn't seen each other for half a century. Walking into the main lounge at the Carlton Nursing Home, Jo-Ro introduces me to a shrivelled character, rug over his knees, half-asleep in an easy chair.

"Stevie," he exclaims once Jo-Ro has coaxed him into consciousness. "What the hell are you doing here?"

"That's amazing," she says. "Sometimes he doesn't recognise his family, or pretends not to, but he's clocked you straight off. Anyway, I'll leave you to gabble for a while."

We chat about old times. I mention the Festival.

"Richmond," he said. "Yeah, when was it?"

"August 1965."

"Yeah. The Who and The Yardbirds. Kipping out on the golf course. What did the locals call us – The Great Unwashed."

"And what about hitchhiking home? With that weird guy in his van."

"Yeah," his face lighting up. "Nearly killed us!"

But after 20 minutes his interest wanes. He flops, his head on his chest, arms dangling by the sides of the chair. I brush crumbs off him, stay there for a while but give up, go to find Jo-Ro.

"That's how it is," she admits. "Do you know, he upset me something awful the other day. Said he wanted to go to Switzerland."

"Surely that would do him good. Mountain air and all that."

She glares at me. "He said you had a strange sense of humour. Haven't you heard of Dignitas?"

We drive away, both quiet. I'm shocked. Dropping me off at the station she clasps my arm, says: "He just needs something to spark him back into life. Something to look forward to."

I promise to think about it.

Kendo is easy to locate. He's long ago abandoned the removals business, has gone all creative. 'Kendo's Original Art Studio' is an old farm building in the English Lake District. He shapes and decorates Lakeland slate and, though in his early 80s, is still hard at it. And he has stayed slim, retaining hair and beard, although grey now and more straggly. Denims, an oversized Guernsey sweater, a brightly coloured neckerchief. His eyes are clear, laser corrected and drug free.

"Not really," he replies when I asked him if he recalled August 1965. "Was on another planet in those days."

"But..." he adds. "If you're talking about that...." pointing through a window to a muddy maroon coloured van jacked up on bricks in the backyard. On the side panels, orange flashes with the logo 'Kendo Your Groovy Mover'.

"Wow, you kept it. And it looks in good nick."

"Well, originally it was a Commer ambulance. Lots of steel in it. Built to last. I used it for hauling furniture around. Couldn't bear to part when I changed tack and got into this slate stuff. Want a brew?"

Over mugs of coffee he tells me of his alcoholism, his marriage break-up – "She took the kids" - and how he found solace in poetry and art. Ivanhoe became a long-term conversion project.

"Thought it would make a great camper, been at it for God knows how long, but I keep losing momentum. Haven't touched it for months. Such a shame. I'd love to get it back on the road."

"I'll come up at weekends, give you a lift with it. It's got happy memories for me."

Six months later I show Dave some images. Kendo

posing by the van, freshly painted, wheels back on. He gets excited. "Yeah, yeah!" Then frustrated, wanting to climb out of the chair, knowing he can't.

"Come on," I say, whipping the rug off him, manoeuvring his wheelchair into position. "Let's get you sorted."

"Why, where we going?"

"For a ride, pal. Just for a ride."

Kendo and Jo-Ro are waiting. As we shove Dave into Ivanhoe he laughs and shouts: "Hope he's got insurance!"

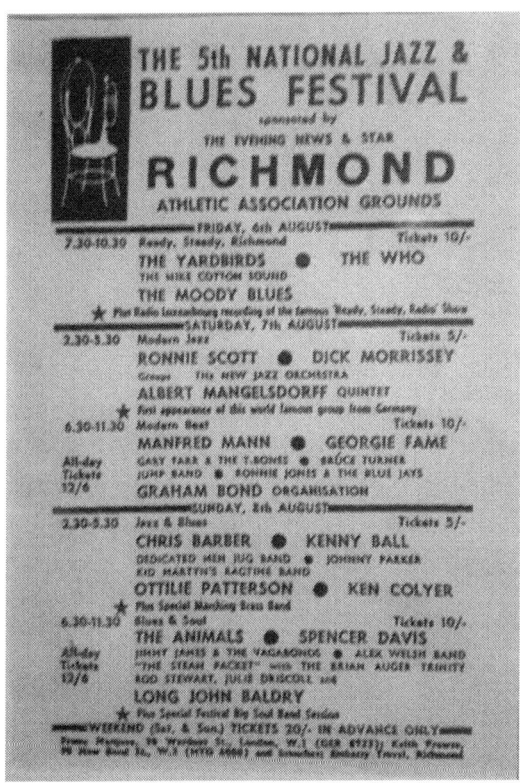

Poster for the Richmond Festival 1965. Note the Friday night set - The Yardbirds, The Who and The Moody Blues. All for 10 shillings! The locals weren't too happy though - they called us 'The Great Unwashed' and their protests of degenerate behaviour caused it to be the last such festival at Richmond.

◆ ◆ ◆

NOTES

A Certain Chemistry: The prompt for this was 'Fool'. I recalled a fictional teacher but also wanted to illustrate the problems of dementia and also how we are all foolish sometimes.

Good Old Mum: In my quiet, picturesque home town was a huge prison, demolished 90 years ago. They hanged murderers there and the cells were cold and lonely. I found a sketch made by a prisoner and wrote the story to go with it.

Miss Stoope's Double Cross Stitch: Inspired by a simple postcard sent in 1907 to an address in 'Richmond, Mo' (Missouri). When I researched the recipient I bumped into wonderful characters like Jesse James and the Silver Princess, Susie Bransford.

A Rough Guide To Slates: Old roof slates are textured with lines of colour and a dozen of them hang from our garden fence. They tell a story.

Voiceless: My book 'No Pity' was a cold case investigation into a brutal and unsolved murder in 1901 when a peace-loving tailor was gunned down for no apparent reason. But Mary Jane, the prosecution's chief witness in the real trial and the central figure in this story was also a victim.

The Dirt: I was a crime reporter for some years in

Manchester, covering all sorts of nasty goings-on. Murders, rapes, gangland turf wars, riots. My first job was a teenager who wanted to 'be something' – so he robbed a bank.

Wings Of Magic: Children can believe in magic. According to legend, the beautiful and rare Clifden moth can provide it.

The Smiling Refugee: Hopefully, this story illustrates two sides of the immigration debate and, even more hopefully, how tolerance, understanding and, yes, some compromise can bring about solutions.

Pariah Dog: Edmund Avery was my g x 2 grandmother's brother. Official records say he and his wife Mary were killed in the Indian uprising of 1857 but maybe Edmund escaped....

The Feathers: You never know who you might meet...when the organisers of this competition gave the prompt 'Feathers' I assumed they were referring to something light and, erm, feathery. I tried to concoct something different.

Death On The Grapevine: Here we meet 'Ged', a larger than life club-owner I might have known. And the hard-bitten reporter I once knew as Colin Evans.

The Squeeze: Ambling along the warm, summer evening street. A pleasant family outing. But suddenly tripwires appear.

Daisy Up The Amazon: Researching something entirely different, I came across an article about a cruise line which plied annually from Liverpool to Manaus in the mid 20th century. An exotic adventure began to form.

Have A Drink On Me: Based on a true incident. If I'd been a journalist in the Edwardian period I would have felt forced to investigate this further. As it was, the full facts never emerged.

Baby Face: Like a lot of this book, a bit of an experiment. This one to show how a short story can be shaved to the bone to creat a much a shorter one.

Travels With Kendo: In August 1965 I and some pals from the North-West of England attended the 5th National Jazz and Blues Festival at Richmond near London and this is a dramatised version of how two of us got back home.

ABOUT THE AUTHOR

Colin Evans

A retired newspaper reporter who covered crime and sport. In recent years he has written a number of books, wide-ranging in time and subject, and now enjoys creating short stories about anything. Hiis family spans four generations and he thanks them all for their tolerance.

PRAISE FOR AUTHOR

NO PITY:
1:'Enthralling - you won't be able to put this book down'.
2: 'A compelling account of one of the most startling murder cases in Edwardian Britain'.

- AMAZON REVIEW

MODS & BLOCKERS:
'.. an amusing, informative and thoroughly enjoyable read by an author who feels deeply about cricket and many other things, but never takes himself too seriously.'

- AMAZON REVIEW

FAROKH - THE CRICKETING CAVALIER
'Purchased for my Father when read it in two days

he could not put it down it was so interesting. Thank you'.

BOOKS BY THIS AUTHOR

The Knutsford Suffragists (Etive Independent)

Describes how a remarkable group of activists fought for women's rights in the Edwardian era. Evans came across their story by accident and discovered how his small home town played a big part in the Suffragist movement.

No Pity (Etive Independent)

A cold case murder investigation with a difference. Evans digs into a dark episode which occurred only half a mile from the home of the young girl who became his grandmother. Yet no-one had ever told him about it....

Farokh - The Cricketing Cavalier (Max Books)

The authorised biography of Farokh Engineer, the

Indian cricket star. A must for cricket lovers.

Mods & Blockers (Max Books)

The summer of 1965 when 'something happened'. A strange mixture of cricket and The March of the Mods.

The Averys Of India

A family memoir centred on the heat and dust - and fascination - of the sub-continent.

Printed in Dunstable, United Kingdom